The LONG TRAIL NORTH

**Center Point
Large Print**

**This Large Print Book carries the
Seal of Approval of N.A.V.H.**

The
LONG
TRAIL
NORTH

Wayne D. Overholser

CENTER POINT PUBLISHING
THORNDIKE, MAINE

This Center Point Large Print edition
is published in the year 2008 by arrangement with
Golden West Literary Agency.

The text of this Large Print edition is unabridged. In other
aspects, this book may vary from the original edition.
Printed in the United States of America.
Set in 16-point Times New Roman type.

ISBN: 978-1-60285-240-2

Library of Congress Cataloging-in-Publication Data

Overholser, Wayne D., 1906-1996.
    The long trail north / Wayne D. Overholser.--Center Point large print ed.
        p. cm.
    ISBN: 978-1-60285-240-2 (lib. bdg. : alk. paper)
    1. Large type books. I. Title.

PS3529.V33L66 2008
813'.54--dc22

2008009491

CHAPTER I

The day following my eighteenth birthday I saw my father murdered and I would have seen my mother raped if I hadn't been lying on the kitchen floor knocked cold by a gun barrel in the hands of one of the Rawlins gang. I think it was Jake Rawlins who hit me, but I was never sure because I had my back to him when I was slugged.

For many boys my age this would not have been as terrible as it was for me. Some didn't have good homes or were resentful of discipline or didn't share their father's dream as I did, but it was very nearly the end of the world for me. I was an only child, and I had been very close to my parents as far back as I can remember.

I was born on a hill farm in southern Indiana, June 1, 1856. We had no money, but my father, Sam Garth, was a great man according to any standard I could think of. I remember two things about our life on the farm: our poverty and my father's dream. He would take me up on his knee and say, "Lane, we ain't always gonna be poor."

I remember my mother, Mary Garth, was a very pretty woman. When I was a small boy I would compare her to other women who went to our church or the sociables at the schoolhouse, and I always decided with satisfaction that she was prettier than any of the others. My father thought so, too, and said it many times.

She laughed easily, and I remember the wonderful sound of her laughter even during times of hardship. Whenever she heard my father say that about not always being poor, she would laugh, not sarcastically and not in any way belittling of my father, but with the fine sound of good humor. She would ask, "Sam, how soon is it going to happen? I want to be ready."

It became a kind of ritual. Maybe neither one believed that it would ever happen because there was no wealth in our neighborhood, and, as far as I knew, no wealth in either family. My ancestry on both sides could be traced back to colonial days, my father's people coming to New York in the late 1600s and my mother's people settling in Pennsylvania in the early 1700s.

The Garths and the Ramsays, my mother's family, moved west, first to Ohio, then Indiana. From what I was told, both families were farmers, pioneers who spent most of their time hunting and clearing the land, and somehow scraping a poor living from the reluctant earth.

I doubt that any of them ever seriously considered being rich. I don't know why it was my father's dream, but it was. Both parents could joke about it, although later it became a driving ambition with my father, and the jokes were fewer as the years passed.

As long as we lived on that Indiana farm, getting rich was not a serious matter. My father would answer my mother's questions with, "Why, Mary, it will happen any day now. I'm looking for my ship to come sailing up the Wabash. Don't you worry about being ready. I want it to be a surprise."

"It will be," my mother would say.

Then she would start singing *"Bound for the Promised Land."* She had a fine soprano voice, and often sang at church and for funerals and weddings. My father loved to hear her sing, and he would sit absolutely motionless and make me sit just as still as he was.

The last two lines of the chorus went like this:

> "O who will come and go with me,
> I am bound for the promised land."

As soon as my mother finished the fourth and final chorus, my father would shout in a great booming voice, "Lane and me will go."

My mother would laugh again and come to my father and kiss him. She would turn and hesitate so he'd have time to reach out and pat her behind. Then he'd say, "You've got to take both of us. That right, Lane? Us men Garths are sticking with our woman, ain't we?"

I'd say, "Yes, but where is the promised land?"

"Out yonder." He'd wave vaguely toward the west. "Just a little ways out there. We'll find it."

I was almost five when Fort Sumter was fired on. My father was one of the first to enlist when Lincoln called for volunteers. The day he left he set me on his knee and looked at me, the corners of his mouth working. It was one of the very few times in his life that I remember his emotions coming close to getting the best of him.

After a little while he said, "I may be gone a long time, Lane. You've got to be the man of the family while I'm gone."

I didn't understand what was happening, but I said, "I'll be a man."

"Good boy," he said, and put me down.

He kissed my mother, the longest I ever saw them kiss, then he walked out through the front door. Later we stood on the front porch and watched the regiment march past, the officers' horses prancing and the men spick and span in their clean uniforms, eyes straight ahead, muskets on their shoulders, flags flying. I saw my father about halfway back, and I'm sure he saw us, but he didn't wave or even turn his head.

I heard my mother whisper, "God, bring him back to us."

Then a sob shook her body and she whirled and ran into the house. My father was back home several times during the war, twice to recover from wounds. One was in his left leg just below the knee, the other in his right side. The first wound gave him a limp the rest of his life, the second smashed some ribs and was a long time healing. Later I noticed that he was always short of breath if he ran or walked fast or worked strenuously for a while. I always thought that the wound in his side was responsible, though I never heard him say so or even complain about it.

How my mother survived those four years with one small boy to help her is something I will never understand, but she did. So did I. I don't think I ever went to bed without my supper. We lacked variety, but we always had enough food to fill our stomachs.

When my father returned home after Appomattox, he was Captain Samuel Garth, thin and darkly tanned and very tired, but he was alive, and that was as much as we could expect after four years of blood-letting.

The first thing my father said after the crying and the kissing were over was, "We're bound for the promised land."

My mother didn't laugh and she didn't start singing. She just looked at him and asked, "Where is this promised land, Captain Garth?"

He made a vague gesture toward the west as he always had when he answered the question for me, "Out yonder, Mrs. Garth."

I don't think he knew where he was headed, but he did know he wasn't staying on that hill farm. He sold it, loaded our wagon, hitched up our team, and we started west. My mother didn't argue. She was never one to argue with any of his decisions, and besides, she was tired of that hill farm, so tired she never wanted to see it again.

As for me, well, it was the greatest adventure of my life. I wanted to see buffalo and Indians, and I didn't have the slightest doubt about getting rich. I knew we would. My father knew we would. My mother wanted to know how it was going to come about, since if we went on out to the Rockies he might just as well stop looking for his ship to come sailing up the Wabash.

"Just a matter of changing streams," he said. "It's going to be on the South Platte."

After we arrived in Denver, he said, "Maybe it will be on Cherry Creek."

My mother had seen Cherry Creek. She snorted and said it would have to be a mighty small ship.

My father tried to find work, but between the limp and his shortness of breath, it was apparent that he wasn't going to be able to do much hard work. The high altitude made it worse than it had been in Indiana. The upshot of it was he didn't find anything in Denver he could do.

He didn't have enough money left from the sale of his farm to buy a business. Too, it seemed to him that Denver was flooded with veterans looking for work, and that the businessmen who had stayed home and made money didn't have much sympathy for veterans. Maybe they felt guilty.

This was one of the few times I remember my father being pessimistic about the future. He drove south along the foothills of the Rockies, not stopping very long anywhere until we reached Trinidad, just north of the Colorado-New Mexico line. There he got a job as a sheriff's deputy, maybe because the sheriff felt an obligation to a veteran who needed work.

Being a lawman wasn't my father's idea of a good job, but he took it, announcing that now his ship would be coming up the Picketwire. My mother had seen that stream, too. Neither laughter nor singing came so easily to her now. She said, tight-lipped, "It must be a canoe."

Optimism had flowed back into my father. He said, "Some canoes are mighty big, Mary. You just watch. It will be loaded to the brim with all kinds of good things. We'll name the canoe the *Bountiful*."

It worked out fine for all of us. My father was an excellent lawman who earned the respect of everyone in the area, both those of Anglo and those of Mexican blood. He hadn't been in Trinidad more than a year until he knew what he wanted: a cattle ranch above town on the Picketwire.

"Sure it will take money," he said, "but we're going to work and we'll do without some of the things we want, and we'll save our money until we find the right spread."

We did, too. When I wasn't in school I worked at anything I could get, from delivering newspapers and running errands for a storekeeper and cleaning out a livery stable to getting a job on a ranch below town.

My mother worked, too. It wasn't so much that she shared the dream as it was the fact that she wanted anything my father wanted, therefore she was willing to do without the luxuries of life to reach his goal. She worked in a hotel waiting on tables and scrubbing floors and emptying chamberpots, and taking a whack at nursing when a nurse was needed. She had no training, but she had a natural talent for it. She was not afraid of sickness and was willing to go anywhere and take care of anyone, and the doctors loved her.

By the time I was seventeen, we had enough money saved to buy a small spread. I was six feet tall, I weighed one hundred and seventy pounds, and I was a good enough hand to earn a cowboy's thirty a month and beans. Too, my father had seen to it that I learned to handle a gun.

"It's a tool," he told me more than once. "As a tool, you can use it on a lot of different jobs."

He didn't want me to work at cowboying all my life and neither did I. I think that in the back of his mind he had a notion that if we never got the ranch we wanted I could make a living as a lawman. I didn't give that notion much thought because I was determined to have the cattle ranch that had been our goal for so long.

That spring I heard about a ranch up the river that was for sale. It was run down and needed work, but I didn't shy away from work, and I knew that even if my father could not work hard, there were plenty of chores he could do on a small spread.

He rode up the river with me to look at it and he liked it, so we turned around and returned to Trinidad. We called at the bank on our way home. The banker, Colonel Thomas J. Munro, had been a great admirer of my father from the time we came to Trinidad.

"Of course the bank will help you, Captain," the colonel said. "I know the place you're interested in. It's a good ranch. Buy it. Stock it with the best cattle and the best horses you can find." Then he looked at me, his eyes narrowing, a small smile coming to his lips. "Son, I hear you're a good hand. You aiming to stay at home and help work this spread?"

"Yes, sir," I said.

My father looked at me with a good deal of pride, I thought, and that made me proud. He said, "Colonel, I've seen a lot of boys, both in the army and here in Trinidad, and I want to tell you that I've never seen a finer young man than my son."

The banker nodded. "I've heard that about him, Captain, and it's one reason I'll loan you any amount within reason."

I felt ten feet tall when we walked out of the bank. My father had never praised me to another man like that before, not in my hearing anyhow, and when the man was a rich banker like Colonel Thomas Munro, it was enough to make me feel good. We bought the ranch and moved onto it the following day. I still felt good, for this was a dream coming true at last.

We bought four horses to go with the two saddle horses we already owned. The cattle that had been on the ranch had been sold or stolen, so we had to restock the range. After borrowing from the bank and paying for the horses, we had about $5,000 in gold which we hid in a sack of flour.

There were plenty of outlaws in the country who jumped back and forth across the territorial line, and we didn't intend to lose that money. We planned to buy cattle from ranches south of us in New Mexico.

My father said we'd keep the money until we'd bought what we wanted, and if any was left, we'd deposit it in Colonel Munro's bank.

We worked hard through May getting the place in shape, so we took a little extra time off from work at noon on June 1, which was my eighteenth birthday. The next day the Rawlins gang rode in from New Mexico.

CHAPTER II

We had spent several days repairing the corrals. All of them were in bad shape; some of the posts were broken off and the gates were so splintered they wouldn't hold either a rampaging horse or cow. I had cut enough posts off the hill south of us to fix up the corrals, and my father had hauled a wagonload of lumber from town.

On the morning following my birthday we were up at dawn as usual and had finished the corral work before noon. It had been extremely dry for several weeks and we had to get water on the hay meadows. I figured we'd spend the afternoon irrigating, but there wasn't much sense in working a few minutes and then having to quit, so we put away our tools and went to the house for dinner about half past eleven.

When my mother saw us come in, she threw up her hands. "Dinner ain't ready," she said. "I never have dinner before twelve o'clock. I expect my men to work until noon."

"You can expect what you like," my father said amiably, "but when your men get done with a job half an hour before noon, we're coming in whether you've got dinner or not." He sniffed loudly, and added, "Something smells good."

"It'll be good," my mother said. "Now you wash up and skedaddle. I'll call you when dinner's ready."

We washed and combed our hair, then went out on the front porch. We sat down and smoked while we waited, admiring the hay meadows and the willow-lined stream and the hill to the south. I'm sure both of us felt good about what we had done and what we planned, even though at present the spread was a small one and we wouldn't have any money coming from the sale of steers for a while. Colonel Munro had said he wouldn't push us, so we could plan for the long run and not worry about paying the mortgage off within the next year or so.

My father looked tired. I said, "You'd better take a nap after dinner. I'll get the irrigation started."

He shook his head. "I'll be all right as soon as I eat."

A few minutes later my mother came out and stood with us, her back to a post. She said, gazing at the meadow, "Dinner will be ready in another minute or two." She was silent for a time, then she turned her gaze to my father. "You look all in, Sam. You'd better rest before you go back to work."

"I was just telling him he ought to take a nap," I said.

"I'm all right," my father said impatiently. "I just need my dinner."

"You'll get it," my mother said. "I've been thinking. I was wrong about us getting rich. We're rich right now. Not just in money. It's . . . well, it seems to me we've got what we've been wanting."

"That's right," my father said. "That's exactly right."

"It took your faith to do it, Sam," she said. "Yours, too, Lane. I guess mine was lacking. The Bible says faith is the substance of things . . ." She stopped, her gaze on the hill to the south. "Somebody's coming."

"Good," my father said. "I saw Ted McGill in town the other day and told him we were fixing to buy a small herd. He told me the XO ranch wanted to sell some cows and he'd let me know." He frowned and chewed on his lower lip a moment. "I don't know why it takes four men to tell us, though. I figured we'd have to go to them, instead of them coming to us."

I could see there were four riders, all right. I was a little uneasy just on general principles. As my father had said, it shouldn't take four XO hands to tell us they had cows to sell. But something else bothered me. The main road leading south into New Mexico was six or seven miles up the river from us, and it seemed strange these men weren't using it instead of a trail that wound through the hills between our place and the territorial line.

I'm not sure why I didn't get my gun from its holster in the belt hanging over an antler rack just inside the front door. I guess I didn't because my father didn't, so the real mystery is why he didn't. He knew better than I did how many riders were in the country. He couldn't have forgotten about the gold hidden in the sack of flour, either.

Of course I'll never know what thoughts went through my father's mind. He rose as my mother said worriedly, "I don't have enough to feed four extra men. I'd better go peel some more potatoes."

My father got up and started toward the barn, not saying a word. I got up and followed him, my uneasiness growing. By this time the riders had reached the bottom of the hill and had started across the meadow straight toward us. They were about halfway between our buildings and the base of the hill when my father said in a choked voice, "By God, that's Jake Rawlins riding in front."

I wheeled toward the house, deciding I'd better get my gun. My father said, "No, Lane. Don't let 'em know we're afraid. We ain't armed. They'll probably water their horses and ride on into town."

My father knew more about Jake Rawlins than I did, having arrested him about five years earlier after a shooting scrape in Trinidad. He was in jail quite a while before they decided he'd fired in self-defense, which probably wasn't true from what I'd heard about the fracas.

Rawlins hadn't been quite as notorious then as he was now, having robbed a good many banks in the last five years, but he'd been famous enough as a hired gunhand, and maybe Trinidad wanted to get rid of him. Anyhow, he left town in a hurry and since then had lived mostly in New Mexico and Arizona.

Before the riders reached us, my father said in a low tone, "The fat one's Pudge Meline. The other two are the Peck twins, Oscar and Bernie."

I didn't know a thing about any of them except Rawlins, but I suppose my father had arrested all of them at one time or another. It did seem that a good many outlaws and gunslicks rode through Trinidad in those days, and a lawman was bound to have some experience with them.

They reined up beside the water trough, as tough-looking as any bunch of men I'd ever seen. Their horses were dusty and sweaty, and the men were equally dirty with about two weeks' stubble on their faces. Their clothes needed patching and the fat one, Meline, wore a bloody bandage around his forehead. They were on the run, all right, but we had no way of knowing how far behind them the posse was. It probably wouldn't cross the line anyway. A Colorado posse would have to pick up the trail.

Rawlins didn't wait for an invitation to dismount, as good range etiquette dictated and as most men would have done. He stepped down and took a long drink of water from the pipe that fed into the trough, then straightened up and wiped the back of a hairy hand across his mouth.

"We're trading our tired horses for some fresh ones, friend," he said. "Make an argument out of it and you're a dead man." Then he took another look at my father, his beady black eyes narrowing, and he began to curse. "It's the Trinidad deputy, boys, damned if it ain't. Look at him, the same God-damned, smart-alec deputy that got the drop on me and throwed me into his stinking calaboose. Now I call this luck."

From the way he said it, I knew we were in for trouble. I took another good look at him and had a queer feeling I was looking at a huge ape. He had a lot of hair on his face, he had little if any neck, and his arms were unusually long. He carried two guns. Don't let anyone tell you that there were no men in the West who carried two guns; though this was the first one I'd ever seen, I saw more later.

"Looks to me like you're on the dodge, Jake," my father said.

"That's right," Rawlins said, "but we can let up now. I figure we shook our posse way back there around Santa Fe, so don't look for nobody to come over the hill to give you a hand."

"I ain't been watching the hill," my father said, then motioned toward the corral that held the horses. "We've got six animals yonder. Take your pick and move on."

"We ain't in no hurry," Rawlins said.

The others laughed. They had stepped down and had their drinks from the pipe, and now began watering their horses. Meline grinned under his bushy mus-tache, the kind of grin you'd see on a kid who was anticipating a cruel practical joke. He was fat, all right. I guess he was the first fat outlaw or cowboy I had ever seen.

"Why did you quit toting a star?" Meline asked. "Get scared of trying to handle hardcases like us?"

"I've handled enough so-called hardcases like you to know there's no future in being a deputy," my father said. "I wanted a business of my own, so we bought a ranch."

The Peck twins snickered. They looked so much alike I couldn't tell one from the other, tall and skinny with long necks and eyes set very close together astride eagle-beak noses. They appeared to be gangling kids, though they must have been older than they looked, twenty at least.

"You're right about there not being no future in toting a star," one of the twins said. "You oughtta try robbing banks. There's a profession that's got a real future."

"He ain't got no future anyway," Rawlins said. "Not any." He turned to his men. "When I walked out of that jail cell he'd locked me up in, I told myself I'd kill the bastard if I ever had a chance, but I never guessed I'd get it this easy."

"I don't figure even a low-down son of a bitch like you would shoot an unarmed man," my father said, and started toward the house.

He hadn't taken more than three steps before Rawlins pulled a gun and shot him in the back. I knew what he was going to do before he reached for his gun. It was in his face, in his little black eyes, and still I

20

stood there as motionless and useless as if I were nailed to the ground, unable to get a good breath.

I came to the instant he pulled the trigger and I started for him. It was a fool thing to do, but it may have saved my life. If I had turned as my father had, I'm convinced Rawlins would have shot me in the back, too. I don't believe he was capable of facing an unarmed man and killing him, but I'm guessing, of course.

In any case, I didn't quite get to him. Meline stood at his side. Maybe Rawlins was watching my father fall and not paying any attention to me. It was like him to savor every second of my father's dying.

Rawlins had ignored me from the instant he'd ridden up and dismounted. He might have given me the second bullet if he had been aware I was rushing him, but he wasn't. Meline took one step forward and hit me on the chin. He wasn't all fat because he had a punch like the kick of a mule. I've been hit a good many times by a lot of men, but I've never been hit harder than I was by Pudge Meline.

I was knocked cold. I don't know how long I was out and I don't know what happened while I was lying there, but when I came to, three of the outlaws were in the house. One of the Peck twins was sitting on an end of the log trough, his gun lined on me.

"You had quite a nap, kid," Peck said. "Just what did you think you were doing, tackling Jake that way? It's a wonder you're alive. Jake Rawlins is a killer."

I didn't say anything to that, but I didn't doubt what

21

he said. My jaw hurt and I sat up and felt of it. My father was lying on his stomach, his face in the dust of the yard. He was dead. I didn't have to turn him over and feel his pulse to be sure of that.

At that moment I didn't feel anything. I guess I was too numb. I tried to think of something I could do. I was sure my mother was in trouble and I had an idea they'd kill both of us before they left just to keep us from identifying them.

I was still thinking about it and getting nowhere when I heard my mother scream. I lunged to my feet and started toward the house. Peck trotted along behind me, saying something about we'd better go see what was going on.

I went through the front door on the run and across the living room into the kitchen. My mother had set the table for four. Two of the men, Rawlins and one of the Peck twins, had started to eat. Just as I came in, Rawlins jumped up and spat out a mouthful of food, then yelled, "You put poison in that grub! By God, if you did . . ."

"I'll take care of her," Meline said.

He already had my mother backed up against the bedroom door. He'd torn her blouse almost down to her waist. She was sick with fear, her face ghostly white. When she saw me, she screamed, "Run, Lane! Get away."

Meline put a hand on one of her breasts, tipping his face toward hers. I yelled at him to let her alone. He turned his head to look at me, his hands still on my mother. I hit him, a good lick right on the chin like he'd hit me, and I had the satisfaction of seeing him go down. That was when I was slugged with a gun barrel by one of the men behind me.

I didn't come around for a long time. When I did, the first thing I heard was my mother moaning. She was lying on her bed, her face to the wall. I got to my feet and staggered to the door, gripped the casing for a moment until the room quit spinning in front of me, then made it to her bed.

"What happened?" I asked. "What did they do to you?"

She didn't turn to look at me. She whispered, so low I hardly heard it, "They raped me, all four of them."

CHAPTER III

I can't describe how I felt. I just stood there staring at my mother's back. She had pulled a blanket over her. The day was a warm one and I wondered how she could bear being covered that way. Strange how my thoughts went to a subject that was of no importance after what my mother had just said and knowing my father lay dead in the yard.

Somehow I could not come to grips with reality. I had the feeling that this could not have happened, that I must be having the most real nightmare I had ever experienced in my life. I wanted to cry out, I wanted someone to shake me awake, to tell me this had not happened. Or perhaps find out it was happening to someone else and I had been a spectator to a horrible event.

Then I heard my mother say, "Sam's dead, ain't he?"

And I heard my own voice answering, "Yes, he's dead."

Still my mother did not move. Her voice had not been enough to shake me out of the trance into which I had fallen. This was no nightmare; this was not happening to someone else. Then, slowly, the numbness began to fade and in place of it I felt a terrible anger and hate.

I told myself I had two choices. I could ride in to Trinidad and tell the sheriff, or I could go after the killers myself. If I did it myself, I had to get started, but I also knew I could not be gone indefinitely with my mother in this condition.

Then I realized the outlaws had probably not gone very far. It had been evident they had come a long way without rest. Even if they had stolen our horses, I did not think they would ride more than ten or twelve miles without stopping for rest. If they had outdistanced the posse as they said, and the posse did not cross the territorial line, the killers would figure they were safe for the time being.

Suddenly I could think, I was aware, I knew I had something to do. I said, "Ma, I'm going after them. You'll be all right. Just stay in bed until I get back."

"You've got to bury your father," she said.

"I won't be gone for more than a few hours," I said. "I don't think they'll go far without stopping to sleep an hour or so, and if they do, I'll catch up with them. They won't be worried about me going after them. They probably thought I was dead."

"Yes," she said. "They thought they had killed you. I thought so, too."

"You stay right where you are," I said. "I don't want them to get clear out of the country."

I turned and hurried out of the room. In the back of my mind there was a warning that I had done the wrong thing in telling my mother I was leaving, and by actually leaving I was doing something even worse. On the other hand, I don't think I was capable of doing anything different. I was driven by an anger and hate that was new to me, a compelling emotion that overpowered logic. I would have hated myself as long as I lived if I had stayed at home and done nothing and the killers had ridden away without any punishment for their crimes.

Picking up my Winchester and Colt, I left the house, dragged my father's body into the barn so the magpies and coyotes couldn't get at it, then looked in the corral and found their four tired horses as I had expected.

The killers had taken four of our horses. I had expected that, too, but I was surprised that they had left two of ours, one of them being my saddle horse, a four-year-old brown gelding named Ginger. I called him that because he had lots of go in him. He didn't look like much. I suppose that was why they left him. He was smaller than average, but to me he was the toughest and smartest horse I had ever ridden. At that moment I thanked God the bastards had left him.

I saddled up, jammed my rifle into the boot, and mounted. The killers would certainly have gone downstream, so I turned into the road and almost immediately picked up their tracks. Only a few people, mostly Mexicans, lived this far up the river and there was very little traffic on the road, so I felt sure the tracks I was following had been made by the men I was after.

As I rode, I watched the tracks in the soft earth. I found them easier to see as I got farther downstream. We'd had a hard shower two days before and the road wasn't gravel. The rain had been a gully-washer east of our place, so the ground had been soaked and the hoof-prints were deep in most places.

Presently I began watching without much conscious thought. The anger and hate had not died in me, but other thoughts began crowding into my mind—perhaps because I could not bear to think about what had happened. The memory was so painful that for a little while I was almost able to blot out the last hour or more.

I began looking ahead and wondering what my mother and I would do. What would she want to do? I doubted that she would be willing to stay on the ranch, now that my father was dead. She might want to return to town. Maybe she wouldn't have any confidence in my ability to run the place.

If I had my druthers, I'd stay right there on the place

and somehow make it pay because it had been my father's dream and I had shared that dream. Of course I knew I'd have to wait to make a decision and that would not be until my mother could think coherently. I wasn't sure when that would be. Maybe never. I'd heard of women who lost their minds because of this kind of thing happening to them.

Then my father's murder began edging back into my thoughts and another question began to nag me. Why had it happened? We had done nothing to deserve it. We had been as ideal a family as it was possible to be, with none of the bickering and even hate that I had seen in other families. As long as I could remember, there had been only love between my parents and for me.

Oh, I could say that my father's choice of work had brought this on. If he had not been a deputy, he would not have arrested Jake Rawlins, and if he had not jailed Rawlins, the outlaw would have had no reason to hate him and therefore would not have killed him, and if he had not killed my father, they would not have raped my mother.

Well, it was a long list of ifs, and it didn't make much sense. Even with the fact that my father had given Rawlins reason to hate him, the chance of Jake Rawlins turning up in his life five years after he had jailed the man seemed a long-odds proposition.

If my father had lived on a major road or railroad, the odds would have been different, but to live in an isolated, underpopulated area like the upper Picketwire valley and have Jake Rawlins ride in with three other outlaws was the kind of crazy accident or coincidence that defied reason.

Suddenly, near evening, I smelled a fire and began looking around for smoke, jumping to the conclusion that the killers were camped nearby. I had ridden past several Mexican adobe houses and I'd seen a coal mine across the river, but right here there was no sign of a house or cultivated field or mine. I did see a grove of cottonwoods along the stream, and now that I was watching closely, I discovered a thin column of smoke rising above the trees.

I rode slowly for a short distance, feeling certain the killers were down there, maybe on a gravel or sand bar beside the water, and that they, out of caution which outlaws observe as a matter of principle, had made camp with the brush screening them from the road.

Dismounting, I tied Ginger to a small cedar, and pulled my rifle from the boot. I was trembling, excited, I guess, about catching up with the men I aimed to kill. For a moment I stood there, breathing hard, and knowing that if I was going to shoot straight I had to get control of myself.

Oddly enough, the picture of my father's body in the dust of the yard was enough to steady me. I knew I could not handle four of them in a face-to-face fight, so I'd kill them from ambush if I could. I did not then, and have never since then, felt the slightest touch of remorse or guilt. They weren't men; they were mad dogs and I would treat them as mad dogs.

I studied the ground between me and the river, noting the scattering of cedars and boulders. I saw I could get close without being seen, or probably could, because I had no reason to think they would have a guard watching the road.

My guess was they had stopped to cook a meal and rest or sleep until dark, and then would move on. They might decide against riding in daylight. Even in a thinly populated country like this they ran a chance of meeting someone who knew them, or if the posse in New Mexico had wired Trinidad about the outlaws riding north, the sheriff would be looking for them. Then I changed my thinking, realizing that after all they might have a man watching the road and I probably could not sneak up on them as I had planned.

I suppose I stood there a good five minutes, turning the problem over in my mind. I could ride on down the road. Somewhere below me I might find a break in the brush and trees and get a clear shot at the outlaws, but they'd probably see me. If they did, and recognized me, they could cut me down before I had a chance to shoot at them.

If I didn't find the kind of opening I was looking for, I'd have to turn around and ride back, or move from the road to the river. If I rode back, again there was a chance they would spot me. If I crossed to the river, I might not find as much cover between there and the road as there was here.

Of course I had to take into account the possibility that they'd have a guard stationed below me somewhere along the road. I was also aware that they might be riding on any time now because dusk wasn't far away.

These two factors decided me. I'd cross to the river right here. If I didn't get a clear shot when I reached the water, I'd work downstream until I did. Maybe I would anyway. The closer I was, the better chance I'd have to get all four of them.

Once I made up my mind I moved rapidly, using every tree and rocky upthrust I could. It must have taken me fifteen minutes to reach the stream, maybe less, although I doubt it because there were a few places where I got down on my hands and knees and crawled because of the sparse cover.

When I reached the willows I must have taken another five minutes worming through them to the water, being careful not to make a sound or disturbance. I did scare a couple of jays out of the cottonwoods. They gave me a raucous scolding, but that was too common to attract the outlaws' attention. Jays always seemed to be scolding somebody or something.

I eased into the shallow water and, standing close to the willows so I wouldn't be seen, I turned my gaze downstream. There they were, all four, on a sand bar just above a bend in the river. If they'd stationed a guard on the road, they had called him in. Even in the fading dusk light, I had no trouble recognizing them. Then my heart began to hammer as I realized I didn't have time to close in on them. They were ready to leave. If I had taken another minute or two, they would have been gone.

Rawlins was already mounted. So was one of the Peck twins. The other twin was holding the reins of two horses while Pudge Meline kicked out the fire. The light was too thin for accurate shooting at this distance, but I'd never have a better chance, so I levered a shell into the chamber and cut loose.

I was trying for Rawlins, but I missed him. The bullet stung one of the horses the twin was holding. The horse jerked away and went hightailing down the river. The second shot may have hit Rawlins. If it did, it didn't hit hard enough to knock him off his horse. He went out of there in a hurry, the mounted Peck right behind him. The other twin climbed aboard the horse he still held and took off after the other two.

That left Pudge Meline high and dry without a mount. My next shot was at the second twin, but apparently I missed. A moment later I lost sight of him around the bend. I took my time with my last shot and I got Meline. He'd started to run downstream, yelling for one of them to come back and get him. He didn't go far before my bullet caught him. He stumbled about three steps and fell forward into the mud at the edge of the water.

I splashed downstream as fast as I could run, figuring that if I hadn't killed Meline, I'd finish him as soon as I reached him. There wasn't any sense in going after my horse because all three would be long gone before I was in the saddle. When I reached

Meline, I turned him over. He was as dead as he'd ever be.

For a few seconds I stood over his body, staring at it and hating it, then I kicked him in the ribs. It was like kicking a slaughtered steer. He was a heavy man, and the kick didn't budge him an inch. All I could do was to stand there and go on hating the bastard, feeling a keen regret that I hadn't got here sooner. If I had caught them sitting around the fire, or lying there asleep, I probably could have got all four of them.

I went through his pockets and found only a jack-knife and a few small coins, but he wore a heavy money belt. I jerked it off the body and pulled his Colt out of its leather. I looked up at the sky and said aloud, "God, I'm going to keep after those sons-of-bitches and kill all three of them if it takes the rest of my life." Then I walked to the road, mounted Ginger, and rode home.

I was uneasy all the way back. Perhaps it was because I had not completed the mission I had set out to do. The West was a big country. I had no way of knowing where the three outlaws would go, and hunting them would be about like seeking the prover-bial needle in the haystack. Not that it was going to keep me from hunting them. I'd find them. The world just wasn't big enough for them to hide in.

Most of my uneasiness stemmed from my worry about my mother. The closer I got to home, the more my uneasiness nagged me. I would have stayed with her if I had known I was only going to get one man. I had hoped to kill all four, but since I hadn't, I might as well have stayed home. It would be about as easy to run down four men as three.

But what was done was done. It was foolish to wish I had done something different from what I had, but knowing that didn't keep me from being foolish. I knew how much my mother had loved my father, I knew how empty her life would be without him.

I was also aware that she knew I was mature enough to take care of myself. She had said something once last year that was almost in those words. I think she was proud that she and my father had raised me to be independent.

By the time I dismounted in front of my house, I had wooled all of this around in my head long enough to be reasonably sure what I would find when I got home. I left Ginger's reins dangling and ran inside, calling, "Ma! Ma!" There was no answer.

I struck a match, lighted the lamp that was on the oak stand in the middle of the room, picked it up, and went across the kitchen into my mother's bedroom. I saw immediately that my worst fears had been realized.

My mother had shot herself. I gripped a hand. It was cold. She had been dead for hours. It was now about midnight, so she must have done it soon after I left. She had got out of bed and gone into the front room; she had taken my father's Colt out of the holster, and returned to her bed. Lying down, she had shot herself through the heart. The gun was on the floor beside the bed.

I stood there looking at her for a long time, or so it seemed to me. There was little resemblance between her face and the way she had looked when she was alive, but I had been around dead people enough to know it was always this way. She looked peaceful, I thought, and then the notion occurred to me that perhaps she was better off dead than to have lived without my father.

Then I wondered if she had gone to the barn and looked at my father's body. That may have been what made her do it. I did not blame myself for letting this happen. I could not have prevented it. No matter what I did, she would have found an opportunity to kill herself. There was no way under the sun I could have been with her every minute of the day. Still, I wished I had stayed. Just having someone to talk to might have helped her.

Turning, I left the bedroom. Outside I found a note on the table. I set the lamp down and read:

Dear Lane,

Your father and me are proud of you and we love you very much. You are young, but you are a man, so I have no worry about you. I hope you will forgive me for what I am going to do. I cannot face the future without your father beside me. I went into the barn and looked at the body, but that wasn't Sam Garth. He's gone and I'm going to him. It would not be fair to you to force you to spend your life looking after your mother. Find a wife, Lane, and have children. The only true happiness you will ever have will come from your wife and your sons and daughters.

Your mother

I sat down and lowered my face to my arms on the table. For the first time since I was a small boy I cried. It was a long time before I could stop.

CHAPTER IV

Later—I don't know how long because I lost all notion of time—I got up from the table, left the house, and put Ginger away. I couldn't sleep or eat. My parents had to be buried and I might just as well get started.

We had no close neighbors. Mexican families lived above us and below us on the river, but the closest one was more than a mile away. I had nothing against Mexicans. It was just that we hadn't gotten acquainted with any of them. They probably would have helped me if I had asked them, or even if I had just told them what had happened, but they weren't friends, so I made up my mind to take care of the burying myself.

My parents did have friends in town. Perhaps I should have taken the bodies to town and had funerals with a preacher and everything, but I didn't want to do that, either. They were my parents, it was my business, and that was why I decided to take care of all of it.

Maybe I was wrong, but I did what I thought I

should do, and I still don't know how you can be sure what's right or wrong, or how anyone can make a judgment about such matters with certainty. In any case, I've never been sorry I did it the way I did.

I lighted a lantern and took it and a pick and shovel to the bench between the meadow and the hills to the south. I selected this place because the first time my father was here he rode to the bench and sat in his saddle for several minutes, not saying a thing, just looking around. Finally he said, "You know, Lane, we're going to buy this ranch and I'm going to live my life out right here. This would be a good place to be buried."

It had been a portent, I suppose, but neither of us had recognized it. I'm sure he expected to live out his full threescore and ten on this ranch. His life turned out to be a short one, but the shortness of time did not detract from his desire to be buried in this place. My mother, of course, would want to be buried beside him.

I worked until sunup on a grave, then returned to the house and built a fire and cooked breakfast. Not that I was hungry. I simply ran out of steam. I rested and smoked a cigarette and drank several cups of coffee, trying to keep my gaze away from the bedroom door. I returned to the bench and finished the graves late in the afternoon. I came back to the house dead tired, but determined to get the job finished.

Two of the six horses we'd had were work animals, but were broken for riding. Actually they were built like saddle horses, and that was no doubt the reason the outlaws had taken one of them instead of Ginger. They had left one of the team, and I hitched Ginger up to the wagon with the horse they had left.

Ginger had been harnessed before, but he'd never liked it and he didn't like it now. It didn't take long to haul the bodies to the graves, then I drove back to the barn, unhooked, and stripped the harness from the horses. Ginger, of course, was relieved.

I found two pieces of canvas in the barn and took them to the bench. I wrapped the bodies in them and then eased each into a grave. I held my composure through this, even to reciting the Lord's Prayer, the only part of the Bible I could remember.

Not that it made any real difference how much of the Bible I remembered. My folks had never been church-goers or particularly religious people, but they were good human beings. I was convinced that was what counted. I knew they believed that, too. I never took any stock in this business of needing to make peace with one's Maker. They had never done anything to disturb their peace with their Maker.

When I began shoveling dirt back into the graves, the tears came again. I couldn't stop them. My parents' deaths seemed such a waste. They were comparatively young and should have had many years of life ahead of them. Again I asked myself the question why, but still there was no answer. Now I sensed that there never would be an answer I could understand.

Somehow I got through it by the time it was dark. As soon as the dirt was rounded up on the graves I went back to the house, dropped the pick and shovel on the ground in front of the porch, and went to bed. I slept the clock around, and when I woke, the sun was well up in the eastern sky.

I spent most of the next day carving headboards for the graves, and set them into the soft dirt at the ends of the graves. Then I hitched up the horses again and hauled enough lumber and cedar posts to build a fence around the graves. Ginger glared at me as if this second insult was simply too much to bear.

"This is an emergency," I told him. "As far as I know, it won't happen again."

I had talked to Ginger from the first day I'd had him, and I had often told my father he understood what I said. I thought he did now. At least he stopped glaring at me and bowed his head as if accepting the inevitable.

I took three days to build the fence, finding that the physical work was good for me and gave me something else to think about. I realized that neither the fence nor the headboards would last forever, but at least the fence would keep horses and cattle off the graves for a time. Possibly after the valley was settled a cemetery serving everyone in the area would be started around these two graves.

The following morning I took the horses the outlaws had left and the gun and the money belt I had taken from Pudge Meline's body to the sheriff in Trinidad. I told him what had happened. At first he was sore because I hadn't come to town right after I'd shot

Meline and told him about it then. He'd had a wire from the New Mexico authorities to be on the lookout for the Rawlins gang. If he had known about them right away, he'd have organized a posse and gone after them.

I didn't want to get into a fracas with him, so I said, "I had to bury my father and mother." I patted the money belt, then laid it on his desk. "I thought you'd want this. I figured the dinero came from a holdup."

"Hell, yes, I want that," he said. "They robbed a Santa Fe bank and beat the posse across the line. No use cussing you about it, I reckon. I'd probably have waited till morning, and by that time they'd have been out of the country."

He hadn't been in office a full year, and my father had worked for him only part of that time, but it had been long enough for him to learn to respect my father and my mother too. And although he didn't know me very well, he had no reason to dislike me. He scratched his chin awhile, looking at me from under bushy black brows.

Finally he asked, "What are you going to do, son?"

"I'm going to see the bank," I answered, "then go back to the ranch, pack up a few things, saddle my horse, and start looking for Jake Rawlins and the Peck twins. I'm going to kill them."

"Where do you figure to start?"

"Dodge City," I said. "I don't know they'll go there. I don't know where they'll go, but I'm guessing they'll head for towns where things are happening.

Dodge City has plenty of things going on. They might figure they'll be swallowed up by the crowd."

He nodded agreement. "That's as good a guess as any. If they ain't there, the chances are good they'll be in one of the other cowtowns." He scratched his chin some more, then blurted, "Damn it, Lane, you're purty young to go sashaying around the country after hard-cases like Rawlins and the Pecks. I wouldn't be doing my duty to your folks if I didn't offer you a home."

"I'm one hundred years old," I said. "I was eighteen the day before my parents were killed. The other eighty-two years have gone by since then."

He nodded as if he understood. I don't think he did; I don't think anyone could have understood, but he didn't argue any more with me.

"All right," he said. "I can't stop you from going after them. Maybe it's something you've got to do."

"That's right," I said.

"There's a five-hundred-dollar reward for killing Pudge Meline. They brought his body in the day after you killed him and his horse was picked up and left at the Red Front Livery stable. I guess he belongs to you. Stop in before you leave town and I'll see you get the reward. You might as well sell them four horses the Rawlins bunch left. They probably ain't as good as the ones they stole, but you'll get something for 'em. I remember that black gelding your pa rode. He's a damned fine saddle horse."

"Thanks," I said. "I'll stop by later in the week."

I sold the horses along with the one Meline had been

riding and then went to the bank. Colonel Munro shook hands with me and motioned to a chair. "Sit down, son," he said. "How are you and your folks getting along on your new ranch?"

When I told him what had happened, I thought he was going to cry. He shook his head when I finished and said, "That's a damned shame. I never knew a man I liked better than Sam Garth. I didn't know your mother very well, but everybody said she was a fine woman. A damned shame. After coming through the war the way he did and then to get killed by an outlaw." He shook his head again. "A damned shame. That's what it is."

We sat in silence for what must have been five minutes, the Colonel staring into space and not seeing a thing, or so I guessed. Anyhow, his expression was vacant. Finally he took a handkerchief out of his pants pocket and blew his nose.

"Well, I guess everything your folks had goes to you," the Colonel said. "I don't suppose there are any other heirs, are there?"

"Not that I ever heard of," I said. "I don't even know of any relatives except some cousins back in Ohio and Indiana."

He formed a steeple with his fingers and stared at me, his mouth firming into a thin line. He cleared his throat and I imagined I could see dollar signs forming in his eyes.

"What do you aim to do, son?" he asked.

"As soon as I can clear up the business angles," I

said, "I'm starting to hunt for the three outlaws. Sooner or later I'll find them and I'll kill them."

"I see," he said as if he expected that. "Now what are your plans about the ranch? As you know, the bank has a large mortgage on it."

That irritated me. He knew as well as I did that the property was worth more than the amount the bank had loaned us. I said, "I don't want to stay around here long enough to sell it. I figured I'd turn it back to you."

"Good," he said. "My job, of course, is to see that the bank is protected. I'll have the papers drawn up right away, and if you'll stop in . . ."

"I'll be here in a couple of days," I said.

I got up and left his office, figuring that if he had really wanted to do what was right, he'd have had the ranch appraised and paid me the difference between that and the amount of the mortgage, but I guess a banker never operates that way. What I wanted most of all was to wind everything up and get on my way. The longer I was delayed, the farther away Rawlins and the Peck twins would be if they kept riding.

I planned to deposit the $5,000 we had hidden in the sack of flour in the Colonel's bank, but I changed my mind. I decided I'd leave it in a Pueblo bank. I didn't want to carry that much cash on me, and I didn't want Colonel Munro to use it to make more money for his bank.

I rode home and spent the next two days going through everything in the house. We had thrown away some of our belongings when we'd moved here, but there were clothes and personal possessions and furniture that I didn't want to leave for someone else to use. Or maybe I just didn't want Colonel Munro making any more money out of me. He'd make enough when he sold this ranch. I couldn't carry many of our things with me, and I doubted that I could sell the stuff for much in Trinidad, so I burned everything I could.

The thing to do, I decided, was to use the second horse for a pack animal. I put aside the grub I thought I could use along with blankets and a few personal items like my shaving gear. I wanted to have some keepsakes that had belonged to my parents, but I ended up with nothing except my father's watch, my mother's wedding ring, and their wedding picture.

I carried everything out of the house except my bed and burned all of it, which meant I had a good fire going both days. On the third morning I saddled Ginger, packed all I intended to take on the second horse, and rode downstream to Trinidad. I left the horses in a livery stable, collected the reward money from the sheriff, dropped into the bank to sign the papers Munro had for me, and then took a room in a hotel.

The next morning I left at dawn, rode to Pueblo, and deposited most of the money in a bank. I kept $500 in my money belt and $20 in my pocket. I didn't have any definite plans beyond going to Dodge City, though I stopped in at all of the saloons in Pueblo and asked if anyone had seen Rawlins and the Peck twins.

Several bartenders knew them, more didn't, but either way none had seen them recently.

Not that I expected to pick up the trail in Pueblo. I just wanted to sow a few seeds. I had an idea that if I traveled over the West long enough and asked in enough places about the three outlaws, the word would get to them that I was looking for them.

The chances were they'd figure out I was the man who had shot and killed Pudge Meline, and maybe they'd get a little scared. It would work to my advantage if they did. As I asked, I let it be known I was going to kill them when I found them.

The next morning I rode down the Arkansas to Dodge City.

CHAPTER V

I was in and out of Dodge City several times in the following years—exciting visits, because in those days Dodge City was one hell of a tough town. I met some of the most notorious men in the West: Wild Bill Hickock, Bat Masterson, Frank James, Wyatt Earp, Doc Holliday, Eddie Foy, Ben Thompson, Luke Short, Clay Allison, and others. Sooner or later it seemed that just about every tough I'd ever heard of came to Dodge City.

I never became good friends with any of them. A good many, like Doc Holliday, had mighty few redeeming traits. I gambled very little, knowing that an amateur like me would lose his shirt to one of the professionals, and I needed my money to live on. I drank even less than I gambled, and none of the whores got rich on my money. The result was I had little contact with any of the hardcases beyond seeing them around town.

As far as money went, I stayed about even on the board, working when I ran behind. I wasn't too proud to take any kind of a job, even to swamping out a saloon or cleaning up a livery barn. As a matter of fact, I purposely took jobs like those because they kept me among people, I heard them talk, and I listened. Now and then I heard some news about the Rawlins gang.

Apparently Jake Rawlins had picked up a new man named Bronco Reel and had held up a couple of trains in eastern Kansas. About all I knew was that they were still in business, and I was as sure as ever that sooner or later they'd show up in Dodge.

When I wasn't working, I'd hang around saloons like the Long Branch, or variety halls like Ben Springer's place. As I said, it was an exciting time and place, and I kept my ears open to all the talk I could. Sometimes there was so much racket it was hard to hear what I wanted to between the click and clatter and banging of dice and balls and wheels, and the constant shouts of men calling "Get your money down, men," or "Keno," or the other calls that go with gambling. The noise didn't let up until well into the early hours of the morning.

Some of the famous men I met were decent human

beings—Bat Masterson, for instance; but others, like Ben Thompson and Holliday, were just plain mean, morose, ill-tempered, and hard drinkers, and I saw no advantage in cultivating their acquaintance.

I had a purpose in living and I was not interested in dying. On the other hand, as I watched some of the most obnoxious hardcases, I suspected that a good many of them were ready to die, having tasted all the carnal pleasures in life they could and finding that even a full meal of such fare did not satisfy a man. I had a notion that they preferred to die with bullets in their hearts than go to prison as some of them eventually did, or die a lingering, painful death from disease as Doc Holliday did.

When I left Dodge City the first time I rode east, making a full circle with stops in Wichita, Ellsworth, Abilene, Ogallala, and Cheyenne. By the time I visited Denver and Pueblo and returned to Dodge City, I had picked up several rumors about the Rawlins gang.

I made it a habit when I first rode into a town to go to the local lawmen and ask if any of the Rawlins bunch had been seen around there lately. Then I would do the same in the saloons, never telling who I was or what I wanted with them. The first summer and winter added up to complete failure as far as finding the men were concerned, but word got around that I was looking for them. I hoped it would become a war of nerves and they'd crack up, and in the end I think that was what happened with the Peck twins.

The rumor that was most persistent was that the

outfit had broken up, that Rawlins and Bronco Reel had headed north to the Black Hills. I was tempted to go after them, but I also heard that the Peck twins were back in Colorado. The weather was bad by this time, with blizzards rolling across the plains. Making the long ride to the Black Hills was strictly suicide, so I holed up in Dodge City for the rest of the winter.

As soon as the weather warmed up, I rode into Colorado and visited all the small prairie towns I'd heard of. Most of them didn't amount to much, but had sprung up along the railroad, hoping to be future Denvers. It was about all my life was worth to get out of some of those towns without buying a dozen town lots. Other settlements had been started where some sharpshooter thought there would be a railroad route, but had missed it. Now they were drying up to nothing.

I never knew for sure what caused the breakup of the gang, but I was inclined to take some of the credit. One story I heard often was that the twins figured I'd show up in some town like Kit Carson or Cheyenne Wells sooner or later, and the smart thing to do was to pick the town and wait there for me. They'd kill me, of course, just to get me off their backs. They'd heard all they wanted to about me asking for them everywhere I went.

Rawlins was a restless bastard, though, and he wouldn't stand still for such a plan. I think he had more guts than the twins anyhow and wasn't worried much about me. Anyhow, there was some rumbling of gold being found in the Black Hills, so he and Reel lit out for the Hills. When I heard that, I was afraid the Sioux would beat me to Rawlins, but the weather was still questionable in the spring, so I decided to find the twins first and then start after Rawlins.

By the first of July I was pretty well known in all of the prairie towns in eastern Colorado. I'd been in Colorado longer than I had intended, but I still thought I'd find the twins. It was like playing blind man's bluff. Sometimes I'd miss them by less than twenty-four hours, which happened in Cheyenne Wells twice and Kit Carson once. I had a hunch all this time that they were hunting me as much as I was hunting them, so I was extra careful, figuring that if they ever saw me close enough to identify me, they'd gut shoot me from the mouth of an alley some dark night.

I had the advantage of having seen them and knowing they were the kind of strange-looking men who could never hide their identity. On the other hand, they didn't know who I was or what I wanted with them or even why I was looking for them. That kept them on the anxious seat, so it was an additional advantage.

I never told any of the lawmen or bartenders I talked to the whole story. All I ever said was that I was not a lawman, that I wanted to see the Peck twins on personal business. That, of course, could be anything from paying them money I owed them to shooting them for revenge. I suspected the men I spoke to were pretty sure it was the latter, because from everything I heard, the Pecks were as ruthless and mean as anyone on the plains. Not that they had any guts. From the gossip I'd heard about them I judged they were the back-shooting kind, which made them even more dangerous than men who would stand and face their enemy in a fight.

They were always careful to stay on good terms with the bartenders, and that, of course, was one of their advantages. Not that I made enemies of the bartenders. It was just that the twins had been in the country longer than I had, and threw their money around, which I didn't.

I suppose the twins had plenty of descriptions of me and my horse, but they thought Lane Garth was dead, so they wouldn't know who I was. I didn't think I looked peculiar enough in any way for them to be certain they could identify me from my description if they did run into me in a saloon or on a street.

I finally caught up with them on the afternoon of July 2 in a little prairie town named Elma. It was one of those sorry, dying towns that a promoter had founded and was going to make his fortune by selling lots. He'd made a bet with destiny that a railroad spur would cut south from Cheyenne Wells to the Arkansas River and he'd lost. I guess a survey had actually been made through that country. Anyhow, he'd staked out the town and sold a few lots, but the railroad never materialized. Now everyone except a few stubborn idiots who believed in the town's future and were hanging on knew the railroad was just a dream.

The day was a hot one. I hadn't found any shade since I'd left Cheyenne Wells. I'd never been in Elma before. As I rode into the town, I wondered why I was here this time. Nobody in his right mind would ever go to Elma of his own free will.

The only reason I was here was because a lawman in Cheyenne Wells had a tip that the Peck twins were holed up in Elma, thinking it was off the beaten track and no one would think of looking for them there. They'd made a pretty shrewd guess at that, but maybe it was a trap and they'd passed out the tip themselves. I wondered, since they were known outlaws, why the lawman hadn't gone after them himself. Anyhow, I felt I had to have a look here, but now I wondered if it was going to be worth it.

There were just three buildings in Elma, not enough to call it a town, and I made a guess that there weren't more than three people in town. One building was a livery stable with a corral behind it, the second was a general store, and the third was a combination hotel-saloon, a two-story structure with a balcony that ran the width of the building. A doorway opened onto the balcony between the two upstairs windows, probably from the hall.

I couldn't see any houses, so I assumed that who-ever lived in Elma must have rooms in the saloon. Across the road a bunch of weather-beaten stakes marked the lots that had been surveyed. Apparently the railroad was to have come on through town a block east of the buildings.

The town reeked of death: decay lay like a dark shadow upon the place. No trees, no grass, and no sidewalks. The street had not even been graded. It was absolutely flat with only the sagebrush scraped off. The dust had blown off, leaving the hardpan, but there was plenty of dust around the town. I had a hunch that when the wind blew, which it did much of the time, the air would be gray with it.

I dismounted and tied up in front of the saloon, then stood there looking around and telling myself I had never seen as dismal a place as this in my entire life, and I had seen a multitude of little towns in Kansas, Nebraska, Wyoming and Colorado, being so much on the move in the last year. For some reason the sense of broken dreams and false hopes seemed greater here than in any of the other places.

None of the buildings had been painted. All of them showed the weathering that comes from wind and sun. A shiver ran along my spine. I told myself again that the town reeked of death, maybe my own if the Peck twins were here and had set up a trap for me. Certainly the death of the town was not far away. Probably within a year the place would be deserted, the windows broken, maybe even the buildings torn down by the nearby ranchers for lumber.

Finally I went indoors. I had wanted to stand in front of the saloon for a moment to show the twins, if they were watching, that I didn't think they were here, and that if they were that I wasn't afraid of them. Besides, it might be cooler inside than it was in the sun; but that was only wishful thinking. If any-thing it was worse inside. The heat was caught and held by the four walls, and it was a stagnant heat that smelled of stale sweat and bad whisky and cheap cigar smoke.

The interior of the saloon was as dismal as the out-side. The bar was a single unplaned plank laid across two saw horses. A shelf behind it held a variety of bot-tles and glasses. I saw one green-topped table, four chairs, a back door, and on the east wall two windows, the glass covered with dust and cobwebs. Even the top of the table was more gray than green from its thick covering of dust. The haunting gray of death was here, too, and I felt it in the pit of my stomach as I crossed the room to the bar and asked for a beer.

The bartender was the only person in the room. He was an old man, gray of hair and gray of face. He fitted very naturally into this strange, haunting town that should have been buried and wasn't. He looked at me for quite a while before he turned and drew my beer, his faded eyes narrowed, his cracked lips squeezed tightly together.

He finally shoved the beer at me, then stepped back and kept on staring at me as if he couldn't make up his mind about something. I sipped my beer and looked around. There was a door in the rear end of the room and a stairway at the street end. If the twins were here, I figured they'd be upstairs. The chances were they had seen me ride up and were waiting for the proper time to make their play. Maybe they expected the bartender to make certain I was the man they thought I was and give them the high sign.

I wasn't quite sure how to work it, but I figured I'd better not hurry anything. I asked casually, "Business isn't real rushing, is it?"

He shook his head. That was all. No movement of his lips. Just that bare, short shake of his head. I glanced at the stairs again, wondering if one of the twins might slip down them and start shooting when I was looking the other way. Was the other twin waiting behind the back door watching me through a peephole to see when my back was turned to him?

I began feeling a little queasy in the stomach, thinking about the possibilities that two men would have from opposite ends of the saloon. As I've said, I'd had a hunch right along that neither of the twins had any real guts. Or brains, either. From what I'd heard, Jake Rawlins was the one with both the guts and the brains. Without him, the twins wouldn't amount to much. Still, it didn't take either guts or brains to shoot a man in the back. I figured that was what I'd better watch out for.

Somehow the bartender would give the twins the signal when he'd made up his mind I was the man they wanted. I watched him as closely as he was watching me, but I just couldn't read his gray, impassive face.

"Does that back door lead into another room?" I asked. "Maybe a kitchen?"

He nodded, a bare, half-inch tip of his head. I'd

guessed that the bartender was serving meals along with the rooms he rented. One of the twins was probably in the kitchen, and the other one upstairs ready to ease down the stairs when he got the bartender's signal.

I had a hunch then. The twins being careful as they were and not very long on guts or brains, I figured they'd play it along, careful like, until the bartender let them know when they could catch me in a crossfire. I was making some assumptions that might be wrong, but I had to figure it that way. The biggest mistake I could make would be to stand here and give them all the time in the world. My game, then, was to explode their scheme quickly before they had a chance to set me up.

I walked casually to the end of the bar, then turned and took two quick steps to where the bartender stood; I caught him by both shoulders and shook him until his teeth rattled. I didn't say anything. I didn't think there was any need to. I gave him a turn so he faced the back of the saloon and, holding him with my left hand, I pulled my gun with my right hand and prodded him in the back with the muzzle.

"Move," I said.

We went straight toward the back door. The bartender didn't make a sound until we reached it, then he began to curse me in a high-pitched voice. I said, "Open it," and dug the muzzle of my gun a little deeper into his back.

He flung the door open and we went in fast. One of

the twins was there, all right, a gun in his hand. I couldn't have mistaken him. He was as tall and skinny and long-necked as ever, the eyes set close together astride that eagle-beak nose.

I'm sure there was a peep hole in the wall and that he had been watching us, but he was still a little uncertain when I lunged into the room holding the bartender in front of me. He fired point-blank at us, but we were moving and the bartender was yelling curses at the top of his voice. The twin must have been nervous, mad, too, I guess, because their scheme hadn't worked out the way they had planned. Anyhow, even at that distance he missed.

He never had another chance. I let him have it in the belly, the big slug knocking him back against the wall. He hung there a few seconds, his mouth sagging open, his trigger finger twitching in the agony of death and slamming a second bullet into the floor; then his feet slid out from under him and he went on down to the floor. I fired a second time as he was going down. I knew I didn't have to worry any more about him. I got him right through the brisket.

I had no way of knowing whether the old man wanted into the fight or not, but I'd have been foolish to have left him standing there with the twin's gun on the floor only a few feet from him. I turned, hit him across the top of the head, and he went down, out cold. I didn't slug him hard enough to crack his skull, but he'd be out for a while, and he'd have a king-sized headache when he woke up.

The back door of the kitchen opened into what would have been an alley if the town had developed. Now it was just a back yard, with several clumps of sagebrush and a dirty mess of old bottles, empty tin cans, garbage, and other assorted junk.

I had to make a decision in a hurry. I could go back across the saloon and climb the stairs, figuring the second twin was up there, or I could go out through the back and circle the building to the front. All I could think was that the second man might come down the stairs as I left the kitchen, or maybe was already down, and would cut me to pieces before I got a shot off. That struck me as suicidal, so I took the alternative. I ran out through the back door and around the saloon to the street.

The second twin was headed down the street toward the livery stable. He must have figured the shooting in the kitchen had gone sour and he'd jumped from the balcony. Apparently he'd boogered up a leg because he was limping.

I yelled at him. He wheeled and fired, the kind of reckless shot that a panicky man would take. It missed by three feet. I cut him down then, though he got off one more wild shot as he fell.

I moved toward him, not sure how hard he'd been hit. He lay motionless on his belly until I had covered about half the distance to him, then his right hand snaked out to grab the gun he'd dropped. He raised himself up on one elbow and tilted the gun barrel up. I shot him again, this time in the head. His arm gave way and his face plopped down against the hardpan. When I reached him, he was dead.

I picked up his gun and threw it as far as I could into the sagebrush, then sprinted back to my horse, got aboard, and headed out of town on the run, not sure who was in the store or the livery stable, or whether they would pick up the fight.

When the town was behind me, I pulled my horse down. I felt no sense of elation about killing the two men; I felt no twinge of guilt, either. It was simply something I had to do and now it was out of the way. I wiped the sweat off my face, took one last look at Elma, and headed north to Cheyenne Wells.

I never went back, but afterwards when I thought about the town, I often wondered whether I could find the places where the buildings had stood if I went back. The place so reeked of death and decay that it couldn't have lasted much longer. I had a hunch that if I did find it, I would see nothing except a few rusty nails, the bottles, the tin cans, and at least two graves.

Now only Jake Rawlins was left.

CHAPTER VI

The second year was much like the first except that I spent most of it in New Mexico and Arizona. I rode to Cheyenne Wells after I left Elma, thinking that if Rawlins and Reel had gone to the Black Hills and returned, Cheyenne was the one place they'd be bound to hit on their way south. If they hadn't come through yet, I'd get a job and wait for them.

The news of the Custer fight had just come in and the handwriting was on the wall and plain to read. The Indians had fought the shoes off Crook in the battle of the Rosebud, and then had won the greatest fight in the history of their long war with the whites in the Little Big Horn affair, but they never had hung together and I didn't believe they would now. Besides, more soldiers would be rushed into Montana and the Dakotas, so while the Indians had earned their moment of glory, they had also decided their own fate.

With the Indian menace out of the way, the rush to the gold fields would be greater than ever. If Jake Rawlins hadn't already left the Black Hills, he might stay there. Too, he could come out through Sidney or Bismarck, but I still bet on Cheyenne, partly because most of the traffic came through that way, and mostly because this had been his country and I figured he'd return to it.

Within a matter of hours after my arrival in Cheyenne, I learned that Rawlins had been here and gone. He was not a man to hide his light under a basket. He hadn't been in Cheyenne twenty-four hours before he got into a saloon brawl, beat a man almost to death, and wound up in jail. Reel was sore about him getting into trouble, and when he found out Rawlins was going to be there a few days, he pulled out.

There were a couple of things here I didn't understand. Number one was why Reel didn't wait for Rawlins to get out of jail, or at least until he knew how long his partner would be in. Rawlins was fined one hundred dollars, and after a week in jail he was turned loose on the promise he'd get out of Wyoming and stay out. By the time I got there he was miles away.

After quizzing several bartenders in the saloons where Rawlins and Reel had done their drinking, I figured out why they hadn't been getting along. Apparently they had quarreled over leaving the Black Hills, although I never heard the details of the row except that Reel had wanted to stay.

If this was true, I suppose Reel was glad to get away from Rawlins and probably hoped his ex-partner would be locked up the rest of his life. The bartenders agreed that Rawlins was in a rage because Reel had walked out on him and had sworn he'd kill Reel when he ran him down. When I heard that, the thought occurred to me that the Sioux hadn't beaten me to the job of killing Rawlins, but his ex-partner Reel might.

The second point that bothered me was why the police hadn't held Rawlins. When I asked the chief point-blank, he didn't give me much of an answer. He looked away and mumbled something about Rawlins not being wanted in Wyoming and they couldn't hold all the outlaws that were wanted in other states and territories.

The gold rush to the Black Hills along with the new railroad going through Cheyenne were bringing most of the known outlaws in the country through there.

The chief said as long as they kept going, the law wasn't going to bother them.

This made me pretty damned mad. I said hotly, "That's a hell of a way to run the law. Rawlins is wanted in at least three territories that I know of. All you had to do was to notify the Colorado authorities and they'd have come and got him."

I'd backed the chief up against the wall and it made him sore. He said, "Kid, you're talking mighty big for your age."

"Age hasn't got anything to do with it," I said. "If you'd just held that bastard till I got here, I'd have killed him and he wouldn't be bothering anybody."

That amused him. He snickered and said, "You? Kill Jake Rawlins? Well, sonny, you'd better wait till you're dry behind the ears before you tackle that hard-case."

That made me madder than ever. I thought about crawling over the desk and poking a fist down his throat, but I didn't, figuring I'd wind up doing thirty days in his jail. It wouldn't be worth it. Instead, I said, "I killed Pudge Meline more than a year ago in Colorado near Trinidad. A little over a week ago I killed the Peck twins in Elma, Colorado. I came here looking for Rawlins to kill him, but you turned him loose."

His mouth sagged open and it took him a minute to get around to asking, "You trying to wipe that gang out?"

"They murdered my father," I said, and let it go at that.

I left town that afternoon, knowing I'd be in trouble if I stayed there. It seemed to me that the police had been afraid of Rawlins or they wouldn't have let him go. Chances were he'd keep his promise to stay out of Wyoming, so it was a pretty soft way out for the Cheyenne police, though they used it often enough, plenty of them figuring it was nothing to them what an outlaw had done somewhere else if there wasn't a price on his head. For some reason there wasn't a reward out for Rawlins. That was something else I didn't understand. Anyhow, he was free, and I started out again to find him. All I knew was that he had headed south.

I didn't pick up his tracks until I got to Santa Fe. There I found out that he'd had a gun fight with Reel and killed him. They called it self-defense and let him go, even though he was wanted in New Mexico. Of course nobody shed any tears over the demise of Bronco Reel. Maybe the Santa Fe police figured that killing Reel deserved a reward, so they rewarded Rawlins by giving him his freedom.

There I was, too late again. And this time Jake Rawlins seemed to have disappeared from the face of the earth. I spent the rest of the summer and all of the fall and winter hunting for him in New Mexico and Arizona. I couldn't pick up his trail anywhere. I saw the southwestern part of the United States, but aside from my new knowledge of geography, I wasted my time.

When the weather warmed up in the spring, I

returned to Dodge City for a few weeks, but somehow the bloom was off the rose. It was as if a big hole had opened up and swallowed Jake Rawlins; I couldn't understand why I found no trace of the man and I heard absolutely nothing about him.

He was the kind of man who was bound to make himself known wherever he was. Publicity was his meat and drink. He was happiest when he was out-fighting, out-smarting, and outrunning lawmen, so for him to hide out somewhere and not attract attention was incredible. I began to wonder if I had failed to read the man correctly. I just couldn't believe that I had, but the fact was he was either dead or holed up somewhere.

He could, of course, have gone to California or north into Oregon, but again that wasn't his country. I just didn't believe he'd leave the Rocky Mountains or even stay away from them for a long period of time.

I realized he could have got sick and died. He might have been killed in a saloon brawl or by the Indians. I knew the Apaches had a grudge against him that went back to the Civil War days. There was a possibility he had been arrested and jailed, but I think I would have read it in the newspapers if he had, as well known as he was, and I made a habit to read the papers carefully.

I stayed in Dodge City until the first of July, hoping he'd show up there, for it still seemed to me the most likely town. When he didn't, I sat down and looked back over the past year of riding and hunting and getting nowhere. I decided it was a bad deal.

Not that I gave up the notion of killing Jake Rawlins for a minute. I'd just find something to do while I waited to hear about him. Sooner or later I would, if he was alive, and when I did hear, I'd start out again.

I could never give up the goal of killing Jake Rawlins unless somebody did it first. I had promised myself and the memory of my parents that I would do it. You don't give up a major goal that easily.

Once I had killed the man, I supposed my life would be without an objective and I'd just drift. I didn't know. I didn't waste much time thinking about it. I couldn't look beyond the day when I'd face Rawlins and let him know who I was and remind him of what he'd done and then kill him.

All I knew for sure was the fact that I had completely wasted my time riding around looking for Rawlins. If I kept on this way, I'd continue to waste my time, at least until I had a lead as to where he was. So I stopped the aimless riding, took my money out of the Pueblo bank, and bought a small spread on the St. Vrain.

In less than a month after I moved onto my ranch, young Morgan Teller came into my life and nothing was the same afterwards. It's strange how a homeless kid like Morg could show up one morning and change the direction of my life. Not that I ever really forgot Jake Rawlins. It was just that killing him became less urgent. Sharing my life with another human being became the important thing.

A man becomes selfish when he lives alone. He

thinks of himself first, plans for himself if it's nothing more important than a meal, and the future becomes a tight and restricted bit of the horizon. We should all die bigger and better human beings than when we came into the world, and living alone doesn't offer the kind of experiences that make a man bigger and better. I guess I got bigger and better after Morg moved in with me, at least I like to think so, but it wasn't because I wanted to. It was because I had to.

I discovered him huddled in one of my haystacks a little after dawn one morning in late August. I didn't have any close neighbors and not many people went through here, the main road from Denver to Cheyenne being a good deal east of my place. Of course I was startled when I found him, shivering and pale and almost buried in the hay.

It irritated me to find him because I didn't like tramps of any kind or age. One reason was that haystacks burned every year because tramps slept in them and smoked. It was just too hard to put up hay to lose it to some lazy, transient bastard who was careless with a match. So I grabbed hold of him by an arm and hauled him out of his nest, prepared to beat hell out of him, but I didn't lay a hand on him. After one look at him I couldn't.

He was the most forlorn-looking kid I ever saw in my life: skinny with hollow cheeks, dirt ground into his face and hands, clothes that were mostly patches on patches and wouldn't have kept anyone warm, a big, crescent-shaped scar on his right cheek, a black eye, and a purple bruise at one end of his mouth.

I grabbed him by a shoulder, my right hand fisted and held back to hit him, but he looked right at me with his one good eye, and said, "I'm hungry, mister."

I lowered my fist and felt about two feet high. I stood looking at him and blinking and trying to swallow the lump in my throat. I didn't know how old he was, but he was sure little. Still, he had a strange kind of old-man look about him that didn't fit his size.

"Come into the house," I said. "We'll have some breakfast."

I strode into the house, asking myself a lot of questions about him, but I put them aside for the moment. He trotted along behind me like an anxious puppy. We went into the kitchen and I pointed to the pump and basin in one corner of the room.

"Wash up," I said. "Breakfast won't take long."

I'd started the fire before I'd gone outside and had set the coffee-pot on the stove. Now I started bacon frying, and when the kid finished washing his hands and face, I said, "Sit down. I'll pour you a cup of coffee."

He did and I gave him the coffee. I started beating up a mess of flapjacks and he sat at the table, sipping his coffee and staring over the rim of his cup at me. I was still having trouble with that lump in my throat.

I tell you he was the most miserable-looking human being I ever saw in my life. He looked as if he hadn't had a square meal for a year. I guess it was that pathetic, grateful expression on his face that got to me.

Being taken in this way and fed was the first kind thing that had happened to him in a long time, I thought.

One thing was sure. He ate a square meal that morning. He wolfed down three times as many flapjacks as I ate and I wondered where he could possibly put them in that skinny body of his. He drank three cups of coffee, and he'd chomp away with his mouth full and say, "This is good, mister." Or, "You're a good cook, mister." Or, "I sure was hungry, mister."

By the time he shook his head when I offered him a flapjack, I was about to pop from curiosity. A kid as little as he was certainly had no business being out on his own. Naturally I wondered what kind of folks he had and where they were. Chances were he'd run away from home, and maybe, with the beaten-up face he had, he had plenty of reason to run away.

I got up and went to the stove and brought the coffee-pot back to the table, figuring I'd get his story out of him. I filled our cups and took the pot back to the stove, but when I returned to the table, he had his head down on his arms and was sound asleep. I didn't have the heart to wake him, so I picked him up and took him into the bedroom and laid him on my bed.

He was about as heavy as a bag of feathers. I stood looking down at him for a while, at the skinny body and scarred-up face and dirt ground into him, and I felt like crying. If I ever got my hands on the bastard who had done this to him, I'd kill him.

I turned and walked out of the bedroom.

CHAPTER VII

I had to wake the boy for supper. He ate that with the same relish he had eaten breakfast. As soon as he finished, I stoked up the fire and filled the boiler with water. I didn't ask him if he wanted a bath. I figured that if he was going to stay here even for a little while, he'd take a bath and get some of the dirt off his scrawny body.

He watched me, but he didn't say a word. I think he knew what was going to happen, all right. When the boiler was filled, I poured coffee into our cups and sat down across the table from him to wait for the water to heat.

"What's your name?" I asked.

"Morgan Teller," he answered. "People call me Morg."

"My name's Lane Garth." I reached across the table and shook hands with him. "If you're going to stay here a day or two, I thought we'd better find out what to call each other. I also thought you'd better take a bath."

I'm not sure he heard what I said about the bath. He stared at me, round-eyed, then burst out, "You going to let me stay with you, Mr. Garth?"

I hadn't thought much about it, except that I did want to get him cleaned up and into some decent clothes, and I wanted to get some fat on his bones. As far as him staying with me was concerned, I hadn't even got that far.

I will admit I was sick and tired of riding around looking for Jake Rawlins, working a little here and a little there, and having no friends and not putting any roots down. I aimed to get square with Jake Rawlins, all right, but I was paying too high a price.

Of course I didn't know the kid well enough to make any permanent deal with him right then, so I shrugged and said, "For a while, anyway. Long enough to get those hollow cheeks of yours filled out."

"Lordy, it would be good to have a place to live," he said.

The boy had a pathetic loneliness about him that got to me. If I didn't watch myself, I'd be offering him a home permanently and he might turn out to be the worst little sneak thief in Colorado. I shrugged, care-less-like, and said, "We'll see, Morg. How old are you?"

"Sixteen," he said.

I almost bit off the end of the pipe I was smoking. I said, "Sixteen?" without thinking how it sounded. The word just popped out. I was that surprised. He looked about ten or eleven.

"Yeah, sixteen," he said, glumly. "I guess I'm a runt, ain't I?"

"You need more grub than you've been getting," I said. "Now tell me where you came from. Looks to me like you ran away from somebody, and that somebody might come looking for you."

"I ran away from somebody, all right," he said, still mighty glum about himself, "and he'll come looking for me, all right, but I ain't going back with him. I'll kill him first. Or kill myself."

"That strikes me as being an extreme solution to the problem," I said. "Go on. Tell me about it."

"Ain't much to tell," he said. "I don't remember my ma at all. I guess she died of mountain fever when I was a baby. My pa raised me, and I ain't got much to complain about him except that he drank too much, him and his partner, Poke Jacobs. He set too much store by Poke, but I'm the one who found that out. Not him.

"They was fifty-niners. I was born the year after they came out here to Colorado. This here Poke is a son-of-a-bitch, but him and Pa got along real good except when both of 'em got too much coffin varnish down their gullets, then they'd get into fights. When that happened, I went somewhere else and let 'em fight."

He stared at his coffee cup for a moment, frowning, then he went on, "I guess I really raised myself. Pa and Poke had a claim on Clear Creek. They'd work it a while till they ran out of money, then they'd get jobs in some big mine till they got enough money to live on for a while. Sometimes that was months 'cause they'd likely as not spend it on that coffin varnish they drank.

"Soon as I got big enough, I had to keep house and cook for 'em. I never got much schooling. I made out purty well until they struck a good vein. They sold out for more money than either one ever seen before. They moved out of the Clear Creek canyon and said

69

they was never going down into a mine again. They bought a horse ranch east of here on Boulder Creek.

"My pa up and died four years ago. When he was still conscious, he told Poke he was leaving his share of the property to him and he was to raise me. That suited Poke fine. He had Pa's half of the ranch and the horses, and I had nothing. He had me to work for him, too, which I have been doing from the day we buried Pa. I guess Pa lived with that bastard for a good part of twenty years without knowing what he was like. If he had, he wouldn't never have given me to him.

"It ain't that I mind the working. I'd rather work than sit on my hind end all the time like Poke does with a jug of rotgut in his hand. It's the beatings I don't like. We ain't never ate very well since Pa died. I reckon that's why I ain't growed. I've tried to run off several times, but he always catches up with me and gives me a hell of a beating, so I got scared he was gonna kill me. I tried staying home, but the last time . . ."

He stopped talking and kind of shuddered. I said, "If that Poke fellow shows up here, we'll see who gets the beating. You'll stay with me long enough to get healed up and enough to eat, then we'll decide what you're going to do."

"Thank you, Mr. Garth." He swallowed and tried to say something, but he ended up by putting his head down on his arms and crying.

As soon as the water was hot, I made him get his clothes off. I poured the water into the washtub, and

70

when I looked at his back, I wished I could get my hands on Poke Jacobs right then. Morg had a pile of scars that criss-crossed his back, along with a couple of raw, running sores that hadn't healed and must have hurt like hell every time he moved.

I didn't really know it at the time, but that may have been when I decided to keep the boy. I do know I told myself that if I ever got hold of the bastard who'd done to Morg, I'd beat him to death. If I'd had my hands on him right then, I think I would have.

I couldn't do much for those sores except to put some salve on them which didn't help much. The next day we rode into Boulder and I bought him some decent clothes and took him to a doctor, who cleaned the sores out and gave me some ointment to put on them. He said they'd probably heal in a few days, that they weren't very deep.

I gave Morg a little black gelding that was just about the right size for him. I bought a saddle before we left town and he rode back home in style, the proudest kid in the country, I guess. I never saw anybody so grateful.

It did me a lot of good just to see the way the boy looked at me. If there was any doubt in my mind before about letting him stay, it was gone by the time we got back to the St. Vrain. The truth was I'd had enough of living alone.

For a week or more nothing happened. I mean, we didn't hear anything from Poke Jacobs. I had plenty of work to do, the place being pretty well run down when

I bought it. Morgan took over the cooking and wood-chopping and fetching water from the river, chores that had taken a good deal of my time. He'd come outside and work with me when he didn't have anything else to do. For a little fellow, he was mighty handy. Even more important to me, I guess, was having somebody around to talk to. If Morg hadn't been there, I'd have started talking to myself.

We hit it off right from the start. You know how it is. With some strangers you're kind of neutral, and there's some you just plain hate without any real logical reason, and then there's some you cotton to. The latter was the way it was with Morg and me.

Of course there were reasons, Morg being grateful to have a home and me wanting somebody around to share my life with, but there was more to it than that, something like gears meshing when the adjustment is perfect.

We never did sit down and talk our situation over. That is, I didn't ask him if he wanted to stay with me and he didn't ask me if he could stay. That was kind of strange, too, but I guess we both had the feeling that this was a partnership which was right and proper and what we wanted.

The only trouble we had was when I made him call me by my first name. He kept wanting to call me Mr. Garth and I knew that was wrong for the way it had to be if we were to have the right relationship. I don't know whether he guessed my age or not. I doubt that I even told him at first.

The queer part of it was that I was only four years older than Morg, but I'd grown up overnight when my parents died. The two years of hunting for Jake Rawlins and killing Meline and the Peck twins added to my years. I had learned by this time that age was not a matter of chronology. Morg was really younger than his years, partly because of his size and mostly because of the way he'd been raised, and I was one hell of a lot older.

In any case, I guess I was more of a father to Morg than anything else. At least in his eyes I was close to being middle-aged, so it was hard for him to call me by my first name. To him it was disrespectful. By the end of the first week, though, he'd got around to calling me Lane without much hesitation.

Both of us knew, I think, that sooner or later Poke Jacobs would show up. He did, riding in one noon just after I'd come in from cutting hay along the river. I don't know what would have happened if he'd got there when I was gone. I'd left both my Winchester and Colt in the house and I'd told Morg to use one of them if he had to. I think he would have. Chances are he'd have killed Jacobs, which would have been a bad thing for him, at least when he got older and looked back on what he'd done. On the other hand, after what he'd told me and after seeing the scars and sores on his back, I wouldn't have blamed him if he had.

It didn't turn out that way, though. I was washing up for dinner when Morg said in a low, dead tone, "Poke's here."

I looked out of the window in time to see a big man get off his horse. Big, that is, if you count fat instead of muscle. The fat was plain enough to see, with a belly that bulged over his belt and jowls as droopy as his belly.

He was carrying a gun, but I didn't take time to strap mine on. I went through the front door in what was almost a run. Morg's sores had just about healed up, but I was thinking about them as I went down the path toward Jacobs.

"You seen a kid named Morgan Teller?" Jacobs asked. "Peanut size? Brown eyes? Dark hair?"

"Yeah, he's here," I answered. "You Poke Jacobs?"

"I'm Jacobs," he said, as if relieved. "I've been looking all over for him. I'm the kid's guardian. He's run away a dozen times and I'm tired of it. The little bastard don't have no reason to run off, and when I get him home, I'll make him sorry . . ."

That was when I hit him. I've hit a lot of men in my time, but I never on any other occasion have had the sense of pure joy I had when I slugged Poke Jacobs. I let him have it in his oversized melon of a belly, and I guess my fist went clear back to his backbone.

The air came out of him in a burst of whisky-smelling wind that must have emptied his lungs right down to the bottom. His mouth popped open and for a few seconds I saw the most agonized expression on his face I ever saw as he tried to suck air back into his lungs, but it just wouldn't come.

I didn't hit him again. I didn't need to. I just reached

out *and* pushed him over. He fell to the ground and lay there, quivering and groaning and fighting for breath. Morg had come out of the house and stood looking down at Jacobs.

I glanced at the boy, and for the first time since he came I saw hate in his face, raw, absolute hate that shocked me. That was when I became sure that if he had kept on living with Jacobs or had been here alone when Jacobs rode up, he'd have killed the man.

Jacobs finally found enough steam to pull his gun, but he was slow getting it out of leather. I kicked it out of his hand and sent it spinning across the barnyard. Morg said, "That's my pa's gun. Poke never owned a hand gun."

"Get it," I said.

Morg walked to where it landed, picked it up, and brought it back. He cocked it and stood looking down at Jacobs, the hate still in his face. Jacobs was scared then, scared all the way down to his boot heels. I guess he figured Morg had plenty of reason to kill him and that was what Morg aimed to do.

"Don't let him shoot me," Jacobs whined, his blood-shot eyes begging me to save him. "Me and his pa were partners for years. He ain't got no call to . . ."

"Quit whining," Morg said in disgust as he stuck the big gun under his waistband. "I ain't gonna shoot you. Get back on your horse and ride out of here. I won't go with you. I'm never gonna live with you again."

Jacobs got to his feet and staggered toward his horse and fell flat on his face in the dust again. I gave him the toe of my right boot in his fat ribs as I said, "Morg tells me you've got his share of the ranch and the horses that were on it when his pa died. We'll be over to see you in a few days. You'd better have it fixed up so you can pay him for his half, or by God, I'll take it out of your hide."

He struggled to his feet again and this time he made it to his horse. He moved slowly, one hand hugging his belly as he struggled for breath. I guess it still wasn't coming easy. He grabbed the horn and steadied himself for a good minute or more, then pulled himself into the saddle and rode off, leaning forward and groaning every time his horse took a step.

"I don't have no real right to any of Pa's property," Morg said, staring at Jacobs' back. "Pa gave it to him for taking care of me, and he's taken care of me for four years."

"Yeah," I said. "Some care."

Morg didn't argue any about it. I didn't really figure Jacobs would make any kind of a settlement, but I didn't want him to stay in the area, thinking he might try dry-gulching us just to hang onto his outfit.

Jacobs was a man I had no use for whatever. I guess I'd tried him and condemned him and I was ready to execute him if he gave me an excuse. He didn't. When we got around to riding over there, he was gone, the ranch was sold and the new owner had taken possession. I was satisfied if Jacobs had left the country and I guess he had. Anyhow, we never saw or heard of him again.

CHAPTER VIII

I finished out the year on the St. Vrain, but I'm not sure I could have if I hadn't had Morgan Teller for company. It took that year to show me I was still fiddle-footed and not ready to put my roots down anywhere.

Morg would have been happy staying right there on the ranch. I think it was the first time he'd ever been happy in his life, and he hated to change anything for fear the contentment he was enjoying would vanish into thin air.

I didn't pay him any wages, but I gave him the black gelding, the saddle I'd bought for him in Boulder, and a Winchester. You'd have thought I'd given him the world all wrapped up pretty in Christmas paper and tied with a red ribbon. He was that grateful, so grateful it was downright embarrassing.

He was always polite, too. I never knew him to lose his temper, not even when he burned his hand cooking a meal. He did almost all the housework, which I appreciated because I hated it, especially the cooking. He kept his end of it up so well he nearly always had a few hours to come outside and help me.

Sometimes I thought Morg was too good to be true, but after the way he'd lived most of his life, especially after his father died, he found living with me close to paradise, and he didn't want to lose it. I don't think he could have stood it if I'd kicked him out and told him to make his own way. Not that I would have done it. I liked him too well.

He grew six or seven inches that year and took on at least twenty pounds. By the time I sold the ranch, he wasn't the same bedraggled, miserable-looking kid I'd found in my haystack. He always used "we" and "us" instead of "I" and "me." I think that down inside him was the awful fear that I was going to leave him. Anyhow, when I told him one evening that I was going to sell out and head north, he immediately assumed I was taking him along, or pretended to.

The first thing he asked was, "Where are we going?"

"Deadwood," I answered.

I'd told him about my parents' deaths and how I'd killed Meline and the Peck twins, and about my hunting for Rawlins without turning up any trace of him for months. Now it was natural for him to ask, "Think we'll find Rawlins up there?"

"I dunno, but I aim to look," I said. "Now see here, Morg. This is going to be one hell of a tough trip. I'm riding Ginger and I'll take one pack horse. I'm not going on the stage, and I don't figure on throwing in with anybody else. It'd be a lot safer if you stayed around here. I can find a job for you with . . ."

"No." We had been eating supper. Now he stared at his empty plate, the corners of his mouth working. A moment passed before he could control his emotions enough to say, "I can take care of myself, Lane. You know that. I might even be of some help."

"Sure you would," I said hastily, "and I'd like to

take you with me, but there's still been some Indian raiding going on along the Cheyenne-Black Hills road. Bands of young bucks who can't be kept on the reservation hit and run if they can find one man or a couple of them, or even a small wagon train they can handle."

"I know that," he said in a cranky tone, "but I want to go with you. Two of us have a better chance of getting through than one."

I wasn't too sure of that, but I wasn't in any mood to argue with him. I did say, "I just want you to do some mighty careful thinking. The Indian bucks are mean. Two men wouldn't have any show against them if we ran into a band of them. Road agents are operating along the road, too, big gangs of them. They're as mean as the Indians. Besides that, there's bound to be some dirty weather. Heat. Dust. Bad water."

He kept staring at his plate. "I want to go, Lane."

"What's there for you in Deadwood?" I asked.

He lifted his head and looked straight at me. He asked, "What's there for you?"

He had me. It was just that I'd had my bellyful of sitting here on a ranch where nothing much ever happened. I said, "Rawlins, maybe." I was lying and I knew it. I was going whether there was any chance of finding Rawlins or not. The truth was I didn't expect to find him. I was just about convinced he was dead or had disappeared into Mexico or maybe South America.

I knew what the truth was. I just wasn't ready to start

79

ranching yet. Maybe I never would. I didn't know. I did know for sure that I was twenty-one years old, and I'd had too much excitement and I'd been on the move too long to stay put on the St. Vrain. I'd got antsy and that was all there was to it.

He didn't drop his gaze. He could be damned disconcerting when he looked at me that way. When he did it, you couldn't lie to him or dodge his questions. He asked, "Give it to me straight, Lane. You figure I'd be a drag to you? That you'd have to take care of me?"

"No."

"Well then, damn it," he said, "take me with you."

"Sure," I said. "I aimed to all the time, but I wanted you to understand that it won't be a rose garden going up the road to Deadwood."

"Did I ever ask you for a rose garden?" he asked.

"No," I admitted, "you never did."

It took me a month or more to sell the place and clean up the odds and ends. I didn't make much on the ranch, maybe wages for the work I'd done cleaning it up. I kept two pack animals out of the horse herd I sold with the ranch. We loaded them with grub and ammunition and started up the road the first week of August.

This was when Daisy Fallon came into my life, as suddenly and unexpectedly as Morgan Teller had. I've often thought about the timing of events and how it affects a man's life. If we'd started a day later or a day sooner, we'd never have seen her. Or if we'd gone a different route, even by a few miles, we wouldn't have run into her.

I don't understand how and why these things work the way they do, but it's hard for me to believe it's sheer coincidence. Sometimes I think our lives are blueprinted for us the day we're born, or even before, but I can't really believe that, either, because it would do away with the principle of free will.

I refuse to accept the notion that everything which happens to us is predestined. Regardless of the philosophical answer to my question, the fact is that Daisy Fallon was an element in my life from the third day we left the St. Vrain. In Morg's life, too.

I decided to miss Fort Laramie, figuring we'd lose a day if we went that way. We had plenty of grub, so there really wasn't any reason to stop, or to go into Cheyenne, either. We angled east, then cut straight north, just about following the Wyoming-Nebraska line, figuring to camp the third night on the North Platte. We stayed off the road, thinking we'd have a better chance to miss any outlaws who might be on the lookout for a small party.

The Indians were something else. When I'd told Morg about the small bands of young bucks who wouldn't stay on the reservation, I thought I was exaggerating, that they'd never get south of the North Platte or come that close to Fort Laramie. It proved what I should have known all the time, that it is never safe to think you know what Indians are going to do. They are unpredictable at best, though I think in this case they were trying to get under the army's hide by raiding so close to the fort. Or maybe they just wanted to thumb their noses at the soldiers and show what they could get away with. Anyhow, we ran into something I hadn't expected.

Earlier in the afternoon I'd thought I heard some shooting. I held up my hand for Morg to rein in his horse, and cocked my head to listen. I knew we were getting close to the North Platte, though a rise in the prairie ahead of us hid it from our sight.

Morg pulled up and we sat there, the boy watching me curiously. I couldn't hear the shooting after we stopped, and when I asked Morg if he'd heard it, he shook his head. The wind was from the west, so I suppose that for a little while it had carried the sound of gunfire. Maybe it was over. I didn't know, but I was uneasy as we rode north.

When we topped the rise, we saw the line of cottonwoods below us in the valley marking the course of the North Platte. That was a sight I expected to see, but the column of smoke upstream was something else. At least it wasn't anything I wanted to see, though I guess I had half expected it.

I motioned to Morg and we touched up our horses, angling toward the smoke. As we approached, I kept my eyes open, thinking that the Indians had done it and that they might still be around, maybe hiding in the brush along the river.

A few minutes later we saw the most grisly sight I had ever had the misfortune to view in my life. Three covered wagons had been fired and were still smoking. Trunks and boxes had been forced open and all kinds of goods from canned food to corsets and petticoats and women's hats had been scattered around. It was the bodies, however, that turned my stomach: three men, two women, and a small boy. Most of their clothes had been torn off, and they had been mutilated something awful. I didn't study them; I didn't want to look at them any more than I had to.

Morgan was hit harder than I was, which was to be expected. We dismounted and I glanced around, still wondering if some of the Indians were hiding in the brush along the river. Suddenly I realized that Morg was throwing up everything he'd eaten in the last week, or so it seemed. After there wasn't anything else left to come up, he bent over for another three or four minutes, retching until he had to grab the saddle horn to stay on his feet.

I walked around the smoking wagons, still not examining the bodies. I was watching the brush along the river, assuring myself the Indians wouldn't stay here once the job was finished. They had taken the horses and guns and whatever they'd wanted from the trunks and boxes, so it seemed logical to me that they'd skin out of here in a hurry, as close to Fort Laramie as we were. Still, I wasn't easy in my thinking about our situation. I had the thought that if any of them were hiding in the brush, we'd be mighty easy targets.

Once I got to thinking along that line, I knew I had

to look. Leaving Ginger's reins dragging, I walked toward the river, my gun in my hand, the hammer back. The river was running high, and the brush right there was thick.

I got scared then, thinking how easy it would be for a few bucks to hide and cut me down before I even knew they were there. I continued telling myself I was jumpy for no good reason; the thought kept racing through my head that they wouldn't stay and risk a patrol of soldiers from the fort running into them.

There I was, reasoning with myself, or trying to, and at the same time telling myself that I was an idiot and the next second a slug would be coming at me from the brush, when I heard a rustling in the dry leaves somewhere ahead of me.

The instant I heard that rustling I jumped to the conclusion the Indians were just a few feet from me and I was a dead man. I hit the ground belly flat in less time than it takes to tell it. I'm sure I had never moved so fast before or afterward. I scurried crablike toward the trunk of a windfall cottonwood a short distance ahead of me.

When I reached it, I lay there motionless, my heart hammering. I wondered if I dared risk going on around the roots of the big tree, or whether I should jump up and take a wild shot at them, or just lie here and make them come after me. I decided that was the smart thing to do when I remembered that Morg was out there in the open beside his horse and so far I hadn't heard any guns.

I turned my head to look. He'd finally gained control of himself, but now he was standing there as if paralyzed, his gaze on the brush, his eyes bulging from his head. Then he saw me looking at him, and he yelled as if he didn't believe what he saw, "My God, Lane, it's a girl."

Of course I didn't believe it, either, but at least it wasn't an Indian I'd heard rustle the leaves. I stood up and shoved the gun into my holster. Sure enough, it was a girl, standing there staring at me. Thinking how I'd been stampeded just now into diving for cover, I felt about two inches high.

CHAPTER IX

The girl was about fifteen, I judged, with blue eyes and reddish-gold hair that was so wet it clung tightly to her head. In fact, she was wet all over. She must have been hiding in the river when the Indians were here, and from the way she looked, hair and clothes dripping, she hadn't been out of the water very long.

I walked around the log, and went on to the girl, moving slowly, not wanting to scare her. I didn't know what to do or say. I stopped a few feet in front of her and saw that her eyes weren't focusing on anything. She had the appearance of a sleepwalker. She must, I thought, still be in a state of shock.

"These your people?" I asked.

I knew it was a stupid question. She wouldn't be here if they hadn't been her people. I still asked it; I just wanted to see if she would talk. She didn't answer by a word or gesture of any kind. I wasn't even sure she'd heard me.

I put an arm around her as I said, "You get up on my horse behind me and we'll take you to Fort Laramie."

She was as stiff as if her whole body was frozen. She stood motionless, glassy eyes staring straight ahead of her in that strange, unseeing way. I tried to propel her toward the horses, thinking I could force her to walk, but she remained absolutely stiff as if she had lost control of her muscles.

I finally just picked her up and carried her to Ginger. Her legs bent at the knees, but the rest of her body remained stiff. I put her down when we reached my horse, wondering how I was going to get her legs spread enough to set her up behind my saddle.

"Trunk," she whispered. "False . . . bottom."

I hadn't thought she knew what was going on, but obviously she was not as completely unconscious as I had thought. She stood beside Ginger, weaving back and forth like a cornstalk in a breeze, but she didn't seem in any danger of falling. I walked past one of the bodies to a cowhide trunk, picked it up and turned it over and examined it. It didn't have a false bottom. I wondered if she knew what she was talking about, or was she out of her head?

She said, her words barely reaching me, "Wooden . . . trunk."

I went on past two more bodies and a pile of woman's clothes to what looked like more of a heavy oak chest than a trunk. It was empty. I turned it over on its side and tapped the bottom. I placed one hand inside and one outside, trying to figure out if there was enough depth on the outside as compared to the inside to have a false bottom. I decided there was.

Morg had walked up and was watching me. He said, "That's it, Lane. There's an ax yonder. I'll fetch it."

As soon as he handed it to me, I began chopping at the chest. I soon saw that it did indeed have a false bottom, but it was well put together, and it took me a while to loosen the heavy boards. As soon as I knocked one free, money started to pour to the ground, some gold, some silver, with the ends of a good many greenbacks visible.

"Pa's . . . money," the girl said.

"Fetch my saddle bags," I told Morg.

He nodded and brought them to me. I got the rest of the bottom boards loose and we started stuffing the money into the saddle bags. I guessed there were four or five thousand dollars there, enough for the girl to live on for a while or to go back East to relatives and still have some left over.

When I returned to the horse and replaced the saddle bags, I saw that the girl was holding to the horn with one hand. Her eyes were closed now. Her grip on the horn began to loosen and she started to fall. I grabbed her in time so she didn't go all the way to the ground. Her joints seemed to be working now.

She had fainted. I thought it was a good sign. Anyhow, she wasn't in any condition to ride behind me, so the only thing I could do was to hold her in front of me. I wanted to get away from this bloody, nightmarish scene before she came to.

"We'll head for Fort Laramie," I said to Morg.

He nodded, still looking half sick. I stepped into the saddle and, carrying the girl in front of me, started up the river. She was hard to hold, partly because she was limp and unable to hold on to me, but mostly because she was a tall girl and hard to balance. Her head kept bobbing up and down on one side and her feet on the other; I just didn't have enough hands. But by the time we'd gone a mile or so, she came out of it. She grabbed with both hands, her eyes wide and filled with terror.

"You're all right," I said. "You're safe. We're taking you to Fort Laramie."

She relaxed, and from the expression on her face, I judged that she was conscious and able to think and probably talk coherently. At least the sleepwalking look she'd had was gone. I didn't press her, thinking that if she wanted to talk, she would.

"They're all dead?" she whispered.

"Yes," I answered. "What's your name?"

"Daisy Fallon," she said. "It was my mother and father and brother, two uncles, and a wife of one of them. We were going to Idaho. My father was going to buy a ranch. He had enough money . . ." Her grip tightened and she cried out, "The money! It's all back there in that wooden trunk. You can't go off and leave it."

"We've got it," I told her. "You said it was in the wooden trunk that had a false bottom. We took an ax and knocked off enough of the boards to get it."

She relaxed and shut her eyes, her grip easing. "I don't remember telling you about it," she said, and then was silent for quite a while. Presently she asked, "Who are you?"

"Lane Garth," I said. "My friend riding beside us is Morgan Teller. We were heading for Deadwood when we saw the smoke, so we stopped to investigate."

"Funny I don't remember telling you about the money," she said. "You could have gone off and left me and kept the money. You're honest or you wouldn't be telling me you had it. I . . . I guess you intend to give it to me."

"Sure I do," I said, a little irritated by her remark about us leaving her and running off with the money, though I guess plenty of men would have done exactly that. "I'll give it to you as soon as we get to Fort Laramie."

Apparently she didn't think anything more about the money. She said slowly, "I just can't remember anything after the Indians left and I got out of the river."

"You came walking out of the brush," I said. "You looked as if you'd been asleep. We found the money and then you fainted."

"I can't remember any of that," she said in a low tone. "I remember a lot of things before like—like Pa saying we'd camp there beside the river and go on into Fort Laramie in the morning. We'd been pushing the horses pretty hard, he said, so we'd best stop early.

"The men started to unhitch, and Ma and my aunt and I went into the brush beside the river. Ma and Auntie returned to the wagons to start supper and I stayed on the bank thinking about taking off my clothes and having a bath, but the river was high and awful dirty, so I decided not to. I started back to the wagons, but before I got clear out of the brush the Indians came out of nowhere, from upstream, I think.

"The men were surprised and didn't have much of a chance to fight. They were all killed in what seemed to be a few seconds. I couldn't think of anything to do to help them. I didn't have a gun, and if I had showed myself, they'd have killed or taken me prisoner, and I guess that would have been worse than getting killed.

"I backed through the brush to the river and got down into the water. I worked in under some willows that hung out over the bank and held onto one branch so I wouldn't be washed downstream. The current was pretty strong there. Some of them came to the river and looked up and down the stream. I saw them coming, so I got all the way into the water and held my breath. They left before I had to take another breath."

It had been close, I thought, and again the idea about timing came into my mind. If her father had gone straight on through to Fort Laramie, maybe the Indians wouldn't have hit them. I knew the fort wasn't far from where they had started to camp.

Or, even if the Indians had attacked them, the three

men might have been more aware of what was happening and perhaps would have had a better chance to have fought the Indians off.

On the other hand, if the girl had not stayed in the brush, but had gone back to the fire to help with supper, she would have been killed. I doubted they would have taken her prisoner if they were intending to move fast, and I was sure that was their intention, being this close to Fort Laramie. Or, if the Indians who came to the river to look around had stayed longer even by a few seconds, they would have seen her when she poked her head out of the water to take a breath.

The whole proposition boggled my mind, but there was also the interesting question of the why of it. I'd never have the answer. Still, it intrigued me and I've thought about it a good deal. Too many things happen this way, with just a little change in timing on either side of an event making all the difference in the world as to how it turned out.

Half a mile or so out of Fort Laramie we met a patrol. I told the lieutenant about it. "Damn the red bastards," he said, tight-lipped. "We'll see if we can pick up their tracks, but by now they're a long ways from here. Tell the colonel when you get to the fort and he'll send out an ambulance to bring the bodies in."

I said I would and we rode on to the fort. I knew damned well they'd never catch the Indians. As someone said, the Sioux were the best light cavalry in the world. The Cheyennes were just as good. The point was that they traveled light and so could move fast, but the cavalry, with heavy saddles and equipment, simply could not move as fast. I've got a hunch the Indian ponies were better, too, considering the use the young bucks made of them.

The first thing I did when we reached the fort was to get a room in the hotel for Daisy. The owner's wife, a pudgy, motherly type, took charge of the girl right away. I reported to the colonel and returned to the hotel, stopping at the store only long enough to buy a tight leather bag with a lock.

I took a room, figuring Morg and I could sleep together for the one night, and told the boy to look after the saddle horses and pack animals. He was a good hand with horses, so I never worried about them when he was taking care of them.

I carried the saddlebags into my room and moved the money into the bag I'd bought. I locked it and left my room and knocked on Daisy's door.

"Come in," the hotel owner's wife called.

I opened the door and, stepping inside, set the leather bag on the head of Daisy's bed beside her pillow. She was wearing a huge flannel nightgown, her face was pale but clean, her hair brushed and braided. When she saw who I was, she managed a small smile.

"I was hoping you'd stop in to see me," she said.

"She's resting and she needs sleep," the woman said, her voice crisp and plainly indicating I should say howdy and get to hell out of Daisy's room. "I've had the doctor see her. He says there's nothing he can do for her. She needs rest."

I looked more closely at the woman this time, noticing that she was big-breasted with a pushy chin, the kind of woman who controls everyone and everything around her. I'd known a few women like her and they always scared me. I don't know why except that when I'd been a small boy in Indiana we had a neighbor woman who looked the same way. When I was little, I always had an idea that she pushed people aside with her chin, and used her huge bosoms to crush into little pieces those who didn't move out of her way. Silly, maybe, but still I was never able to combat this kind of overbearing woman, so I turned to the door.

"Mr. Garth," Daisy called, "I want to talk to you. Alone." She paused and repeated, "Alone, Mrs. Jitter."

I started to admire Daisy right then because she had spunk. She wasn't afraid of Mrs. Jitter and she let the woman know it. I thought it was kind of comical, watching Mrs. Jitter look at me as if she didn't trust me worth a damn, then at Daisy, and at me again. Finally she rose from her chair and sailed out of the room like a frigate with all guns blasting.

I pulled a chair up to Daisy's bed and asked, "Do you know how much money was in that trunk?"

"Four thousand, eight hundred and ninety-two dollars and twenty-two cents," she said. "The twenty-two cents belonged to my brother."

"I've put all of it in that bag," I said. "You can carry it easily. You can lock it, too." I'd forgotten about the key when Mrs. Jitter tried to run me out of the room. Now I laid it on the bed beside the bag. "You'd better count the money and see that it's all there."

She shook her head again and managed that small smile. "I trust you, Mr. Garth. I'd trust you with my life after you brought me here and handed the money over to me. My mother used to say that if a man was honest in money matters, he was honest in everything. My father didn't agree, but I don't think he knew men as well as my mother did. She'd been married twice before she married Pa."

"You've got enough to take care of yourself," I said. "You'll be taking the stage to Cheyenne and getting on a train and going back to where you came from."

"No, Mr. Garth," she said. "I don't have anybody or anywhere to go back to. That was what I wanted to talk to you about. All of my family were in those wagons. Now they're dead. I'm alone. It's something I never thought was possible. Neither did my parents. I'm . . . I'm scared. I don't know what to do."

"I'll stop in after supper and take your money to the hotel safe," I said. "I wish you'd count it."

"No," she said in a determined voice. "Leave it here."

"About your future," I said. "You've got to decide for yourself, but you can't live here. You'd better go to Cheyenne and from there to Denver if you'd rather. At least you can live on what you've got and go to school for a while."

"I can't live by myself, Mr. Garth," she said, reaching out and taking the hand of mine that was closest to her. "That's what I've been trying to tell you. I've never been taught to take care of myself. I want you to buy me a horse. I'll ride to Deadwood with you. Teach me how to live by myself."

I rose, pulling my hand from hers and thinking that was about the silliest idea I had ever heard. "No, I couldn't do that," I said. "It's a long, dangerous trip to Deadwood. You'll make out all right."

She shut her eyes and tears began running down her cheeks. She whispered, "I wish I'd let them kill me the way they did my parents."

I tiptoed out of the room and shut the door behind me. I went downstairs, feeling mighty low. She didn't know a thing about me except that I hadn't stolen her money. It was just that she didn't have anyone else, so she had turned to me thinking she could trust me with her life. But she'd asked the impossible. What could one man and one boy do with a girl all the way to Deadwood?

CHAPTER X

I didn't say anything to Morg about the girl at supper. After we finished eating, I said, "We'd better roll in. I want to head out of here before sunup."

He looked at me across the table, his eyes kind of squinched up as if he wasn't sure what he ought to do. Finally he asked, "What about the girl?"

"What girl?"

"Daisy," he said impatiently. "Daisy Fallon."

"Nothing about her," I answered just as impatiently as he'd answered me. "She's safe here. All she needs is some rest. That was what Mrs. Jitter said."

"She needs more'n rest," Morg said. "She can't stay here, neither. You know that as well as I do. So does she."

"I told her to go to Cheyenne or Denver to live," I said, irritated with Morg and not understanding why he was talking this way. "Or she can go east on the train if she wants to. She's got plenty of money."

I stood up and reached into my pocket for a cigar, figuring the matter was settled. As far as I was concerned, it was, but not with Morg. It was the first time he'd ever knocked heads with me. I'd always called the shots and I couldn't understand why he was dragging his feet over a girl we'd never seen before and probably would never see again.

"Lane," he said, "this ain't right."

Real anger stirred in me then. I bit off the end of the cigar, fighting my temper. I wanted to reach out and slap him across the face. This had been my decision. He had no business questioning it. The truth was, I guess, that I was irritated because I was worried about the girl, but I still had no intention of being saddled with her all the way to Deadwood. Just because we'd maybe saved her life and had brought her to Fort Laramie didn't mean I was responsible for her from here on out.

"She'll get along," I said, still having a hard time holding my temper down. "Anyhow, we can't drag her all the way to Deadwood with us. You ought to have sense enough to know that."

"No." He shook his head. "I don't have that much sense. We can do it. I think it would be good for both of us to have a girl around. She could keep house for us. I ain't gonna do it after we get to Deadwood. I'm gonna get me a job."

"Stay here and take care of her if that's what you want to do," I said.

"Not by myself," Morg said. "I ain't much older'n she is. You're a man. You could do it. If you don't cotton to the idea of having her ride with us, send her to Deadwood on the stage. She can find us after she gets there."

I started to light my cigar, but I didn't. I blew the match out and put the cigar into my mouth. I chewed on it for about thirty seconds, staring at Morg and seeing the hostility that was in his eyes. In all the time Morg had been with me, we'd never had any hard words. I couldn't understand why we were having them now. Then my temper exploded.

"The girl is not riding to Deadwood with me," I said, "and I am not putting her on the stage. Now, by God, if you don't like it, don't come with me."

I wheeled around and stalked out of the dining room. I stopped in the lobby long enough to light my cigar and then left the hotel, knowing I had to walk my anger off. For the first time since I'd taken Morg I was sorry I hadn't given him his walking papers that first day. Of course it was too late now. I was fond of him, though, and hoped he'd be riding with me in the morning no matter what he thought. After I ran this over in my mind for a little while, I knew I wasn't really sorry I'd let him stay.

I walked to the fort, going past the post sutler's store and around the parade, and on down to the bank of the Laramie river. I stood there and smoked, staring at the slow-moving water and wondered how in hell I had ever got myself into this mess without even trying. I'd been happy just having Morg around. Why he'd picked up the cudgels for Daisy Fallon was more than I knew. It didn't make the least bit of sense.

By the time I got back to the hotel, I'd made up my mind that if Morg opened his mouth one more time about Daisy, I'd tell him we were through. He was big enough and strong enough to make his own way. He didn't need me and I didn't need him.

He was in bed when I went into the room. In the morning he got up when I did, had breakfast with me, and saddled up when I did. We pulled out just as the sun was poking up over the eastern rim of the prairie without a word being said about Daisy.

Morg was pleasant enough, talking along about how this would be great cattle country someday when the Indians were settled down for good, and how he would hate to be a soldier after seeing a few of them around Fort Laramie with nothing much to do except drill and clean the stables and stand guard.

I managed to be friendly, I think, though I'll admit it went against the grain. To my way of thinking, he'd got out of line, and my anger flared every time I remembered how he'd tried to saddle me with the girl and force me to do something I didn't think I could or should. It just hadn't been his place to try to manipulate me that way and being fond of him didn't keep me from being damned resentful.

Regardless of how much I castigated Morg in my thoughts, the real trouble was exactly what it had been all the time. I was using Morg as a scapegoat, trying to blot out my sense of guilt. Whenever I started thinking about the girl, I wondered how she was going to make out. I'd always remember how she'd begged me to take her to Deadwood and asked me to teach her how to take care of herself.

No matter how many times I assured myself that she'd be all right and it wasn't my responsibility to take care of every boy and girl I ran into, I couldn't quite free myself from a sense of guilt for not doing more for Daisy than I had.

For one thing, I didn't feel good about leaving her with Mrs. Jitter, and for a second thing, I realized how tough it was for a girl who had never learned to look out for herself, to get along especially in a wild country like this, and in a fort filled with a bunch of soldiers who usually thought any female was good for only one thing.

I was mighty careful all day not to say a word of this to Morg. I'd never admit to him that I had any second thoughts about my decision. I rolled it around in my mind, but the part I understood least was why Morg had risked my riding off and leaving him in Fort Laramie.

Why had it become so important to him to have the girl go to Deadwood with us? He hadn't known her more than a few hours. She couldn't possibly mean anything to him. It wasn't just a matter of getting a housekeeper. At least I didn't think so. Maybe he didn't really know himself. Anyhow, I wasn't going to ask and open up the whole sad business again.

We crossed the new iron bridge over the North Platte, our horses' hoofs ringing sharply on the planks in the cool morning air. From here the road led north across the rolling Wyoming hills. I had heard that in wet weather this road was a son-of-a-bitch and I could believe it. We'd had dry weather for quite a while, so mud wasn't a problem. The dust was, but it was a minor nuisance compared to what the mud would have been.

I suppose that many years ago the general route that the road followed had been marked by the immense buffalo herds that rolled across the prairie. Certainly the trail had been cut by Indian travois, and possibly later by the Red River carts, though I'm not sure they were ever this far south. Recently there had been the freight outfits moving between Fort Laramie and Fort Pierre; and now the wheels of Concord stage coaches and the covered wagons of pilgrims seeking their fortunes in the Black Hills were cutting the ruts a little deeper, or moving to one side or the other if the ruts became too deep.

We passed a lot of traffic on the road, and met some, too. A few men were on horseback, but most of them were in wagons. We saw stage coaches wheeling south, and I couldn't help wondering how much treasure they were carrying.

We didn't see many women, but that was understandable. New mining camps didn't appeal to women, not the good women, anyhow, and I guess plenty of the other kind had already gone to the Hills. A new mining camp always attracts the bad ones, of course. It was a common saying in the camps that the miners mine the gold and the women mine the miners.

We rode past countless prairie dog towns; we saw herds of antelope some distance from the road, their hind ends shining like white flags. Morgan remarked again about the buffalo grass being good pasture, even though there was plenty of soapweed along with the scattered clumps of cactus. Before we reached the Raw Hide buttes, we spotted a herd of buffalo west of the road. We were tempted to kill one, but decided not to because we didn't want to be held up. Besides, it would have been a waste because we couldn't do much with the meat.

We rode by the Raw Hide Buttes stage station, and later passed the Running Water station, noting the Cardinal's Chair which I had heard about, a stone formation which was greatly eroded now, but was the kind of landmark that the pioneer travelers always talked about.

By the time we reached the Hat Creek station we decided we'd gone far enough. We had seen another buffalo herd just before we reached the station, but again put down temptation, although Morg said wistfully that the way the buffalo were going, there wouldn't be any left in a few years and maybe he'd never get a chance to kill one.

The Hat Creek station was more pretentious than most of the other stations we had seen. Jack Bowman, who ran the place, had a butcher shop, a bakery, telegraph and post office, a blacksmith shop. He sold hay, grain, and food to travelers.

The main building was a solid log structure, and although I didn't see it, I understood that Bowman had dug a tunnel to Sage Creek. He had lived on the plains long enough to know there was still danger of Indian attacks, and the tunnel would guarantee them a water supply if they were under siege.

We stayed in Bowman's hotel, putting our horses in his barn. I talked to a stage driver that evening. He told me Deadwood was settling down, though it was still wild enough. He was uneasy about the trips he was making to Cheyenne, saying bands of hostile Indians occasionally attacked the coach, and the country swarmed with road agents who were more dangerous than Indians. He was bitter about the outlaws, claiming that the driver and shotgun guards were the first to be shot and the government just wasn't giving the protection along the Cheyenne-Black Hills road that it should.

The guard, who had been in the stable, joined us. When he heard what we were talking about, he nodded somberly. "By God, you ain't telling the half of it, Sid. Every time I get to Cheyenne, I swear it was my last trip. There's more thieves and killers on this road then there are honest men. The minute we pull out of Deadwood, my guts tie up into a knot and they stay that way till we pull into Cheyenne."

"If a real treasure coach goes through," the driver said, "they put a young army on board. That makes it purty expensive for the road agents to tackle."

"So they hit the regular runs," the guard went on, "when there's just a driver and a guard. Of course the damned outlaws figure it's easy pickings. There's bound to be a little money in the box and they'll get some off the passengers. They don't hit the jackpot that way, but it's safer'n tackling a treasure coach."

"There ought to be ten times the soldiers patrolling this road than we've got," the driver said bitterly. "Sometimes I think it's like it was in the Alder Gulch days. Maybe the lawmen are in cahoots with the road agents."

"The big trouble is that Cheyenne's the county seat," the guard added. "By the time they get a posse out of Cheyenne, the road agents are a hundred miles away."

"It's a tight organization," the guard said glumly. "Now you take before the Black Hills rush, there was a bunch of horse thieves that worked from here to the

Jackson Hole country and on west into Idaho. East of here into Dakota, too. When the rush started, they concentrated on this road and took to robbing stages and travelers instead of stealing horses. A lot of the killings we blame on the Indians are really done by the road agents."

The driver was looking at me intently as if an idea had just hit him. "What are you gonna do when you get to Deadwood?" he asked.

"Find a job," I said.

"Going prospecting?"

"Not me," I said. "Let the other fellow dig it out of the ground. I'll make mine some other way."

"You're smart." The guard nodded approvingly. "I watch these crazy bastards working every daylight hour scraping what gold they can find out of the ground, then they come into Deadwood and blow it on a whore or lose it bucking the tiger."

"Can you handle a six-horse hitch?" the driver asked.

"I don't know," I answered. "I never tried."

"Can you use a gun?"

I nodded. "My dad was a lawman. He saw to it that I could."

"We're having a hard time holding our guards," the driver said. "You could get a job quick enough."

"Good pay and a quick trip to boot hill," the guard added sardonically.

"I'll think about it," I said.

That night after I was in bed I did think about it. For a short time I had forgotten Jake Rawlins. I never forgot him for long, but selling out and getting started and running into Daisy Fallon and my row with Morg over Daisy had been responsible for putting Rawlins out of my mind. Now he was back.

Remembering what the guard had said about an organization of horse thieves, I began to wonder if Rawlins could be a part of the outfit. Maybe even the leader. He was that kind of man and I didn't think it was likely he would be willing to ride along with the outlaw pack just as another member of the gang.

I don't think I ever believed he was dead. If he had gone to Mexico, I was reasonably sure that sooner or later he'd be back. This was a big operation along the Cheyenne-Black Hills road, obviously profitable, the kind of operation that would appeal to Jake Rawlins.

If my reasoning was right, the quickest way for me to find Rawlins was to get a job as guard. He wouldn't know me. If he wore a mask, I wouldn't know him. If he didn't, I would. In any case, I made up my mind before I went to sleep. I'd apply for a job as shotgun guard as soon as I got to Deadwood.

Deadwood was just about what I had expected, a booming mining camp with ten thousand or more people either in town or in the nearby gulches. I'd heard it was three miles long and fifty feet wide and that description wasn't far off. I could hear the sound of pick and shovel, of rocker and sledge, and I saw innumerable sluice boxes and ditches in the gulches.

The houses surprised me as much as anything. I expected to see the shacks and cabins, but some of the houses were two-story structures, nicely painted, with bay windows and small panes of colored glass in the doors. On the other hand, the main street was exactly what I had expected, narrow and crooked and lined with all kinds of businesses, the majority of them saloons or gambling halls or variety theaters.

We stabled our horses, and after an hour's search, we were lucky enough to find a room in Mrs. Gribble's boarding house, one of the better places, or so we were told. After supper that night Morg suggested we start looking for a house to rent or buy and begin first thing in the morning. I didn't favor the idea, saying that if he wasn't going to do the cooking and such, we'd better just rent a room and buy our meals.

"Where?" he demanded.

"I don't know," I said, "but there must be some decent eating place in Deadwood."

He snorted. "Yeah, like Mrs. Gribble's. One of the better places, you said. I'd sure hate to eat in one of the poorer places."

"You said you weren't going to keep house any more," I said. "Maybe you think I'll take over the cooking."

"No, I'll cook if I have to," he said. "I'm a better cook than Mrs. Gribble and all the others, too, probably. I know one thing. If I have to live on sow belly and beans and coffee that'll take the lining right off my stomach, I'll be glad to cook."

I agreed to it then. We spent the next two days looking for a house both in Deadwood and the surrounding gulches, and we finally found one for rent late in the afternoon of the second day. It was on Williams Street, which had been dug out of the side of Forest Hill on the west slope of the gulch.

One of us was born lucky, I guess, because there were mighty few places of any kind for sale or rent. This one was a tight little house, small and unpainted, but adequate, with two bedrooms, a small kitchen, and a living room. It would do. I don't know what Morg was thinking, but I had no intention of spending the rest of my life in Deadwood.

"I'll get started right away on painting the house," Morg said as we walked back to Mrs. Gribble's boarding house.

We went in, and the instant I stepped through the front door I stopped, flat-footed. Daisy Fallon sat in a rocking chair in Mrs. Gribble's living room, the leather bag I had bought her in Fort Laramie on her lap.

She smiled brightly when we came in and stood up as if she had been expecting us. As she started toward us, she said, "I thought it was about time you two got here."

CHAPTER XI

I should have expected Daisy. She was a determined girl and Morg was a determined boy. Not that I'd have had it any other way. It was just a fact. I guessed right off the bat that they had put their heads together in Fort Laramie, but I didn't say anything about it.

I'd had all the trouble with Morg I wanted over Daisy, and I'll admit that I was glad to see her alive and well. The first glance I had of her wiped the sense of guilt right out of me. If she had gone to Cheyenne or Denver as I had suggested, I'd have wondered all my life what had happened to her.

"You come up on the stage?" I asked.

She nodded. "It's a long ride, but I'm rested now and I feel fine."

"We rented a house today," Morg said with pride. "You got here just in time. You can help pick out the furniture we're gonna buy."

"Why should she help pick it out?" I asked. "She doesn't care what kind of furniture we use."

"Sure she does," Morg said. "She'll be helping use it if she keeps house for us."

I wasn't going to buck her, but I wasn't going to let it go by quite that easy, either. I said, "Aren't you a little previous, Morg? You don't know she wants to keep house for us. She probably wants to look around. Chances are she could find a job that'll pay more than we can."

"Oh, no, Mr. Garth," Daisy cried. "Of course I want to keep house for you. That's why I'm here."

"Maybe you ought to look around first," I said. "Hard to tell what you might run into. Maybe one of these rich miners will hire you as a governess for his kids."

Tears began forming in her eyes. She said in a low tone, "Mr. Garth, I don't want to be a governess. I'm

108

too young even if I did. All I want to do is to keep house for you and Morgan. Won't you let me try? Don't think I'm lazy just because I'm young. I'm a good cook, too."

"Don't cry, Daisy," Morg said. "He's just trying to hooraw you."

I was, but I didn't want Morg telling me I was. The anger which had been so near the surface flared up again, but I was damned if I was going to argue any more with Morg, so I said, "We'll give it a go, Daisy. We'll decide on your wages later."

"I don't want any wages." Tears were running down her cheeks now. "I just want to work for you. I want a home, Mr. Garth. I don't have one any more. I guess you know that."

Suddenly I was ashamed of myself. Not that I had any intention of giving every girl we ran into a job keeping house for us, but Daisy needed help, and if I was going to keep the peace with Morg I had to hire her. I was sorry I'd made it hard on her. Impulsively I put an arm around her and hugged her.

"All right, Daisy," I said. "Any way you want it. Now Morg and me will go wash up. Supper ought to be about ready."

"We had stew last night," Morg told Daisy. "I found one piece of meat in mine. Tonight I guess we get hash. Maybe if I'm lucky I'll find another piece of meat."

I was halfway up the stairs to our room when he caught up with me. He said angrily, "You made her cry, Lane. Damned if you didn't."

I clamped my jaws together until we were inside our room. I pulled off my shirt and washed in the bowl on the bureau, then poured the water into the slop jar. I kept telling myself I was not going to quarrel with Morg any more.

I'd had five days to think about it and remember about my months of knocking around alone, long enough to know that if I had to take Daisy to keep Morg I'd do it. By this time I realized that all three of us had the same problem. Each of us was alone and needed someone to love and care for and think about, so maybe each of us could do something for the other two. But I wasn't ready to say that to Morg.

"You must be in love with Daisy," I said, running a comb through my hair. "It's the only way this whole shebang makes any sense."

"No." He shook his head as he picked up the pitcher and poured water into the bowl. "It's just that I know how another kid feels who's alone in a damned mean, lowdown world and doesn't have anybody to care about what happens to him. I felt sorry for her right from the first. She was like me when you found me in your haystack. She'd got to the end of her rope and she didn't know what to do."

He sloshed water on his face while I dug a clean shirt out of my war bag. I hadn't really thought about it that way before. I'd been raised to take care of myself just as my mother had told me in her note the day she died. I could have done it, too, and before I was as old as Morg or Daisy.

The truth was I didn't fully understand how either of them felt because I wasn't like them and I never had been. I did have sense enough to know that people aren't the same. Their feelings were valid whether I understood them or not. Morg had been beaten and starved; he had been undersized and weak, and somehow I guess he understood Daisy's feelings in a way I couldn't. She hadn't had the trouble he had, but she was a girl, so I suppose the future seemed even more frightening to her than it had to him.

He threw the water out and dried his face, looking sideways at me as if trying to figure out how I felt. Finally he asked, "You ain't mad at me, are you, Lane? I just figured she could do something for us and she sure needed something done for her."

"No, I'm not mad," I said, knowing he'd taught me a lesson I wouldn't forget. "You two got your heads together, didn't you?"

He shot a glance at me, trying to make up his mind whether to lie or tell the truth, I guess. After a while he nodded and said, "Yeah, I talked to her when you left the hotel after supper. You know, Lane, if you hadn't given me a home, I would have killed myself, I think. I wasn't going back and I wasn't going to run no more. I had a notion Daisy was in the same fix.

"She just didn't have anything or anybody to go back to, and she couldn't bring herself to start running. That's why I told her to take the stage to Deadwood as soon as she felt like riding. I figured she could find us in one of the hotels or boarding houses. She did, too."

I hadn't fully understood until then how much I had done for Morg. I scratched my nose and looked at him a moment, then I said, "It'll work out fine if she can cook, but you'd better make up your mind about one thing. We can't pick up every stray boy or girl or dog we run into."

"No, sir," he said quickly. "I know that. I'm satisfied."

We went downstairs and had supper. It was hash just as Morg had said it would be. I was lucky that night. I found the piece of meat. I was certain of one thing. Daisy was bound to be a better cook than Mrs. Gribble.

I will say one thing for Mrs. Gribble. She was a decent human being even if she couldn't cook. She didn't have an empty room, but she fixed a pallet in her bedroom and Daisy slept there that night. We had beds up in our rented house before it was dark the next day, and we stocked enough groceries for Daisy to cook a meal.

That first supper told us we had not made a mistake. Daisy was an excellent cook. I told her I didn't savvy how it was with her after she'd told us her parents had not taught her to look out for herself.

"That's right, Mr. Garth, but . . ."

"Lane," I interrupted. "Let's not start off with so much formality."

"All right, Lane," she said. "I didn't tell you the

whole truth about my family. I did say that my mother had been married twice before she married my father. Well, you see, he wasn't my father. He was my step-father. It was just that Mamma told me to call him my father."

I shrugged my shoulders. "I'm not picky, Daisy. If you called him your father . . ."

"No, it's important, Lane," she said. "I want you to get it straight. My mother wasn't a good woman the way people think of a good woman. She loved me and took care of me, so as far as I was concerned, she was a good woman. It's just that she had a lot of men in her life.

"My real father wasn't any good, either. He was a gambler. He ran off and left us when I was a child. My mother was living with another man when she heard that my father had been killed in a brawl in Denver, so she married the man she had been living with.

"It wasn't long until her second husband was killed, when his team ran away. For several years my mother made a living for us by cooking in different restaurants and boarding houses. She was an awful good cook and she taught me. She kept telling me there were several ways a woman could satisfy a man, but one of the best was by being a good cook."

"She was a pretty smart woman," I said.

"I don't know about that," Daisy said gravely, "but she did know men. She married her third husband about a year ago, the one who was killed by the Indians. He was an antsy kind of man who couldn't stay in one place. He wouldn't listen to anyone, either. He knew it all. I guess that was why he got killed.

"Plenty of men told him to throw in with a bigger outfit, that the Indians were still raiding as far south as the North Platte, but he said it was all hogwash, that after General Miles and General Crook had been chasing them around the way they had, the Indians wouldn't be that far from their reservations, so he sold his store. He got his brothers together and we all started out for Idaho."

I didn't say anything. Neither did Morg. We both sensed, I think, that Daisy wanted to get this off her chest and it was best just to let her talk, so we kept still.

"I'll tell you why that is important, Lane," she said. "You see, I got some real strong notions about men and women from the way my mother lived. She didn't have any morals. She wasn't happy, either. I guess that was the reason. I've seen her go from one man to another, a dozen of them besides the ones she married, but none of them satisfied her. She kept chasing them, and all the time as soon as I was big enough to understand, she warned me not to live the way she always had."

Daisy looked straight at me then, and added, "I'm not going to, either. Any way is better than hers, but I know a lot of women who have taken her way because they think it's the only way to keep from starving to death, or maybe it's just the easiest way. That's why I was determined to follow you and work for you."

She lost me then. "I guess I don't savvy."

"I judged you to be a decent, moral man," she said with great feeling. "If I'm wrong, I want you to tell me, and I'll leave here right now. I think I learned from my mother how to judge men. You could have taken advantage of me. You could have stolen my money. When you didn't, I thought I would be safe with you. Morg, too."

She got to me when she said that. I hadn't thought much about how decent women judged a man or what they expected. I knew where to find a woman who put a price on herself if I wanted one, but I wasn't a man to take advantage of a good woman. I honestly think most men I had met since I'd started traveling by myself were like me.

There weren't many men like Jake Rawlins. They were just notorious, so it always seemed that there were more of them than there actually were. It struck me that this was the kind of man Daisy's mother had been attracted to, so Daisy had got her ideas of men from them. Besides, Daisy was more child than woman. A man who would take advantage of her was an animal, not a man.

Well, I sat there at the table, with Morg looking at me and Daisy waiting for me to tell her what kind of a man I was. I didn't want to claim anything for myself because I didn't deserve it, but I didn't want to go into all of that right then. I thought of something else, too. I didn't want Daisy to think I was going to take care of her for the next ten years.

Finally I got my thoughts shaped up and I said, "Of course you're safe with us. I never had a sister. Neither did Morg. So that's what you'll be."

For a while I thought she was going to cry again. The corners of her mouth trembled and she dabbed at her eyes with her handkerchief, then she got up and came to me and kissed me on the cheek. She went over to Morg and kissed him on the cheek, too.

"I never had a brother, either," she whispered. "I'm glad to have two."

Suddenly I had a crazy notion that I was looking into the future and I saw I would be taking care of her for the next ten years. It wouldn't be easy to get rid of a sister. But I didn't push the point. I was happy to let it stand. The future could look out for itself.

"You're a good cook, Daisy," I said, "and that's the Number One talent for a sister to have. Tomorrow Morg and I will buy the rest of the furniture we'll need. You make a list of all the groceries you want, the kind of stuff that will keep. Dried fruits and canned goods and the like. Staples like flour and sugar and rice. We'll buy them, but after we get jobs, it'll be up to you to buy the groceries. Tomorrow you go find yourself some more clothes. You can't get along with just one outfit."

She nodded agreement, smiling a little as if all of a sudden her future had come secure. She said, "Yes, brother. You're the oldest, so we'll take your orders."

I couldn't argue with that. I'd made a bargain. I had a family to support whether I'd asked for one or not. I

116

wasn't so sure right then that my future was going to be what I wanted. Maybe part of the trouble was that I didn't know what I wanted. I'd never thought past the time when I'd kill Jake Rawlins.

CHAPTER XII

Before the first month was out I made a discovery that amazed me. The three of us were a family. We just seemed to fit. I had a strange, almost haunting feeling that we had known each other for many years. Or in some previous life. That sounds crazy, but when I thought about taking in a boy almost a year ago and more or less adopting him, and now a girl I had never seen until a few weeks before, I began to wonder if we were all crazy, especially when I realized how well we got along with each other.

Daisy had one thing in her favor, just as Morg did. She wasn't the least bit lazy. She seemed happiest when she had something to do. It was her house to care for, the kitchen belonged to her, and she wanted no help from either Morg or me. For a girl, she was unusually capable and dependable. Her mother may not have had any morals, but she'd done a good job raising Daisy.

She was like Morg in another way. She had never known a happy home. I gathered that she hated all the men her mother had lived with. Sometimes I suspected she hated her mother. I'm sure there had been a great deal of bickering between them, so, like Morg, she was so grateful at being given a place to live and could call home that she was determined not to do anything to upset her situation.

It was, I'm sure, a happy situation for her. I often heard her whistling or humming while she cooked a meal or washed dishes or cleaned the house. As far as Morg and I were concerned, we were more than happy, both knowing we would never find another housekeeper as willing and efficient as Daisy. Having briefly tasted boarding-house cooking, we wanted no more of it.

Morg found a job in a few days working with horses for the stage company. The company must have owned hundreds of horses and was constantly buying more, because some were retired due to illness or accidents, some simply became too old for the hard work they were called on to do, and others turned out to be too slow.

Morg's job was to break them to work in harness, or help other men do the breaking. The strange part of it, to me at least, was that he was better than the older, more experienced men. It wasn't long till he was promoted and given a raise in pay, and some of the others were fired.

As for me, I got a job as a shotgun guard on the Cheyenne-Black Hills stage coaches without any trouble, just as the driver had told me I could that evening at the Hat Creek station. Later in the winter I was laid off for a while, but I was soon hired as a night policeman.

Both jobs were fine for me because it didn't take any close listening to hear a good deal of talk about road agents. I suppose some was gossip, but I'm sure a good deal was true. I was fairly certain that Jake Rawlins was in these parts if he was alive. I couldn't believe he was staying away with so much gold being shipped to Cheyenne. Still, I never heard him mentioned.

I liked Deadwood just as I had liked Dodge City, so I didn't mind working and living here while I waited for Jake Rawlins to show up, as I had a hunch he would sooner or later. In fact, Deadwood was similar to Dodge City in several ways: a boom town with plenty of money, whores, gamblers, and sneak thieves to give the good citizens their share of trouble.

Too, Deadwood had its characters just as Dodge City had had. I still heard talk about Wild Bill Hickock being shot to death by Jake McCall even though it had happened the year before. There was Colorado Charlie who had been Hickock's friend; Calamity Jane who was in and out of Deadwood a dozen times in the two years I lived there; and Buffalo Bill Cody, of course, who seemed to turn up sometime or other in just about every town in the West.

Many of the odd characters were not as well known nationally, though they were famous enough locally, men like the notorious gambler Tendie Brown, the gunman Jim Levy, the con man Doc Biggs, Dirty Shirt Brown, Swill Barrel Jimmy, and many others. But no Jake Rawlins, until the spring of 1879, although I'm confident he had been in the country before that. I just hadn't heard about him, so he must have changed from the old Rawlins who had a loud mouth and took pride in being known, to a silent outlaw who shunned publicity.

Morg brought the first hint that Rawlins was in the Black Hills. One night at supper late in the spring of 1879 he said, "Lane, was Rawlins ever known as Bald Jake?"

"I don't know," I said. "I never heard him called that, but that doesn't prove anything either way. Why?"

My heart began to pound, the hope coming to me that maybe my long hunt was over. Morg knew something or he wouldn't have mentioned it. This was well into my second year in Deadwood and I'd been thinking about moving on.

Morg hesitated, not at all sure of himself. Finally he said, "There may not be anything to it. I didn't know whether I ought to mention it or not, but a couple of men were hanging around the company barn today. I didn't know either one of 'em, but they both looked like tough hands. I overheard one say something about Bald Jake, and a little later I heard the name Rawlins. I'm not even sure there was any connection."

"There probably was," I said, "but I'm guessing he's not going to show his face in Deadwood."

I was wrong about that. A few days later I was making my rounds after supper, working at the time as a night policeman, when I saw a black gelding tied in front of the Melodeon saloon. I glanced at the horse casually as I moved along the boardwalk, then stopped and looked at him more closely.

I had a haunting feeling that the animal was familiar. For a moment I wondered why. I had the same feeling I'd have when I passed a stranger on the street who looked like someone I knew. It struck me that this gelding resembled my father's saddle horse which Jake Rawlins had stolen.

That had happened almost five years ago, and I had seen dozens, maybe hundreds, of black geldings during those five years. Still, horses are like people in the sense that no two are exactly alike, even though they look similar.

I'm not sure why the notion struck me that this was the same horse my father had owned, because normally I would have gone on past the animal without a second look. He had not been cared for the way my father had taken care of him, if it was the same horse. He certainly had not been fed well. He was skinny, his ribs showing, and he hadn't been curried for a long time.

Still, the longer I stood there looking, the more I was convinced that this was the horse. It was possible he recognized me. His ears tipped forward and I had the notion he was trying to tell me he knew who I was and I should know who he was. Perhaps it was this hint of recognition on his part that made me stop and study him.

I spoke to the horse and stepped around the hitch rail and patted his neck. I had never ridden him much, but I had helped care for him and had even helped break him to ride. My father loved horses and, having raised him from a colt, had babied him so much he had thought he was a member of the family. He was, too, as much as a horse or dog can be a member of a family.

The black turned his head and nuzzled me. He had the white stockings my father's horse had had, and then I remembered the scar on his left shoulder from a barbed wire cut he'd received the day we moved to the ranch on the Picketwire. I had a hell of a time finding it because he still had his winter coat and, as I said, he hadn't been curried for a long time. When I eventually found it, I knew then beyond any doubt that he was the same horse.

I stepped back on the boardwalk, my heart pounding so hard I found it difficult to breathe. My first thought was: *Jake Rawlins is in Deadwood.* Then my second thought slowed my heart down considerably: *He might have sold the horse or it could have been stolen from him.*

If I had been sure that was the case, I would have waited until the owner showed up and then bought the horse if possible. I'd never thought as much of him as my father had, or as I'd thought of Ginger, but he deserved better care than he was getting from his present owner. Besides, I had a feeling I owed him something just because my father had loved him. On the other hand, if Rawlins was in town, I wanted him and I couldn't wait. It didn't take me long to make a decision. I set out to find Jake Rawlins.

By this time I was well known in all of Deadwood's saloons and gambling halls and brothels, having been called to most of them at one time or another to arrest a troublemaker or stop a fight that was about to get out of hand. Even if I wasn't called, I visited these places almost every night just as a matter of principle.

Maybe I was too well known. Some of the bartenders were friendly with the tough element and I wasn't trusted or liked by them because I represented the law-and-order faction and therefore was an enemy. When I asked about Rawlins, I got lies for answers, or, at best, evasive answers which told me nothing.

Most of the bartenders said they hadn't seen a man who answered the description I gave, and all of them said they had never heard of a man named Jake Rawlins. I wasn't surprised at that because Rawlins had spent most of his time south of the Black Hills. Too, he had not been written up in the newspapers for the last three years. The truth was he just wasn't known up here.

I spent the first half of the night asking questions. I was interrupted twice by requests to make arrests. One concerned a quarrel over a poker game which resulted in a professional gambler shooting and wounding a miner who had called him a crook. The other time I was called to a brothel where a drunken cowboy was threatening to tear the house down because the girl he wanted had left town and he was sore at the madam because she wouldn't tell him why the girl had left or where she had gone.

It was after midnight when I got to the Palace, which was next door to the Melodeon. The bartender was one of the few in Deadwood I trusted and one of the equally few who liked me. He said, "I don't know any Jake Rawlins, and I never heard the man I saw called by name, but this fellow answered your description. He was in here most of the evening, sitting at a back table with a bunch of men who were doing a lot of drinking."

The bartender scratched his head and hesitated, then he said, as if he was really afraid to say it, "You know, Lane, a lot of hardcases have drifted into Deadwood and they always come into a saloon. Well, I never seen a tougher looking bunch of men in my life than these birds. They looked like they'd cut your throat for nothing but the pleasure of doing it. I noticed this particular man you're asking about because he's like you said. He reminded me of a big ape."

"When did he leave?" I asked.

"I dunno," the bartender answered. "Maybe an hour ago. The whole gang got up and left together. Their horses were tied in front of this place and the Melodeon. I noticed they headed south. That's all I know about 'em."

I stood there and looked at the bartender, having some pretty mixed-up feelings about the whole business. I'd been looking for Jake Rawlins for almost five years, and this was the closest I'd come. I had missed him by an hour!

If I had started my search here when I first spotted the horse, I'd have found Rawlins sitting at that back table with the rest of his bunch. But there was the other side of the coin. I'd have jumped him and maybe I'd have killed him, but the rest of the outfit would have taken me on. By this time I would have been a dead man.

"How many were in the gang?" I asked.

The bartender shrugged. "I didn't count 'em, but I'd say six or seven."

He scratched his head again, staring at me. I figured he had something else to say and was scared to say it. He had good reason to be scared. If the toughs found out he'd talked to a lawman, they would have made it hot for him. He finally decided to go ahead.

"Lane, there was one thing I left out. It was another reason I noticed this gent. He looked like a bullet had taken a big chunk out of the left side of his face. He had the damnedest scar I ever seen on a man. It started at the left end of his mouth and angled up clean across his face to his ear.

"It made me kind of sick to look at him. He was that ugly. The scar twisted the whole left side of his face so he had a kind of lopsided look. I had a funny feeling about him, like his face was a jack o'lantern some kid had cut to look scary. By God, his face was scary. I got so before he left I wouldn't look at him."

I didn't know what to think about that. Maybe he'd been shot in a fight and almost killed and laid up all this time, though I didn't think it would take three or four years for a wound like that to heal. I wondered if Bronco Reel had given him that scar when Rawlins killed him in Santa Fe.

When I'd inquired about that fight, no one told me Reel had wounded Rawlins, but that didn't prove anything. Nobody in Santa Fe who had seen the fight wanted to talk much about it. Folks in New Mexico knew Rawlins too well to gossip about anything he was mixed up in. But then he might have got the scar afterwards. He was the kind who invited trouble, so it was hard to tell when he had been wounded. It could have been anywhere.

When I went outside and checked the hitch rail in front of the Melodeon, the black gelding was gone. I knew he would be, of course, and I was sorry because I had hoped I could buy the horse, but then I couldn't have got him from Rawlins. Even if I had killed him and survived the fight, I probably could not have proved to anyone that the horse rightfully belonged to me.

I told Morg and Daisy about it at supper the next evening. Morg said, "That bunch was planning a holdup."

"What makes you say that?" I asked.

"It's no secret," Morg said. "The spring cleanup will be going south before long. Some coach will be carrying $200,000 in gold, maybe more. It's worth taking a chance on. I'm guessing, but I think that outfit got together to plan the holdup."

That much gold was enough to boggle a man's mind and more than enough to make a road agent drool. But the coach would be well guarded. I didn't think much of Morg's notion. Still, Rawlins had the guts and the imagination to try a job that big, so I couldn't really discount what Morg had said.

"What you heard in the company barn was right," I said, "but I still can't figure where Rawlins has been all this time and why he's stayed out of Deadwood."

"I can guess," Daisy said. "He's ashamed of the way he looks, so he's kept out of sight. Maybe his gang has got used to him, but other people would be like the bartender. They'd look the other way."

"It might be," I agreed. "He never was a beauty, but he didn't have a face that made you sick or reminded you of a scary jack o'lantern."

"I don't see what would bring him to town, though," Daisy said. "They could plan a holdup wherever they're staying. He didn't have to come to the Palace with his men."

"Probably a conference of some kind," I said. "Maybe they had to talk to some go-between here in town. I don't think a man living in town would have the guts to ride out into the Pumpkin Buttes country or up the Cheyenne to the road agents' hangout."

"I don't blame 'em," Morg said. "It'd be like visiting a bunch of rattlesnakes in their den." He nodded at me. "Your notion about a conference is probably what brought Rawlins in, all right. The company suspicions that somebody in the organization is a spy. At least I've heard some talk about the road agents getting tipped off when a big shipment of gold is going out."

I'd heard similar gossip, but I hadn't taken much stock in it. That kind of talk is always around when road agents are busy, and they had been most of the time since we'd come to Deadwood.

As I made my rounds that night, I kept asking myself where Rawlins would hide out. I'd light out for any place where I thought I'd find him no matter how risky it was. I'd waited far too long now to kill the bastard. The real trouble was I'd never be a really free man until I'd done it. I hadn't been sure before that he was still alive. Now I was, and I felt the old, familiar impatience prodding me again.

I had no sound idea where he'd be. The country west of the Cheyenne-Black Hills road was big and empty, and the outlaws could find dozens of places to hole up. I'd heard stories about various hideouts and had discounted most of them as being tales that grew with the telling by drunks around the Deadwood saloons. Some of the yarns I'd heard claimed that the James boys were hiding out in eastern Wyoming and were masterminding the holdups. I realized there was a slim chance it was true, but I didn't believe it.

I had just about decided by the time I went off duty early that morning that I'd quit my police job and start riding. It wasn't reasonable, but it would beat sitting here and doing nothing until Rawlins took a notion to disappear again.

But I didn't do anything of the kind. Not then anyway. I hadn't gone fifty feet before I heard my name called. I wheeled and reached for my gun. I guess I was jumpy now that I knew Rawlins was somewhere around. Then my hand dropped away from my gun butt when I recognized Phil Ogle, the stage company's division superintendent.

"You're wanted, Garth," Ogle said. "In the company office. Ron Blake is waiting to talk to you."

CHAPTER XIII

I walked back up Main Street with Ogle. Ron Blake was the stage company's superintendent and part owner from Cheyenne. I'd met him in both Cheyenne and Deadwood. He had been here on several occasions, riding in a two-horse buggy to inspect the road and the various stations along it. I didn't know him well, but I respected him, both from my slender personal acquaintance with him and by reputation. Although I had no idea what he wanted, I certainly was willing to talk to him.

I followed Ogle into his private office. Blake was sitting at Ogle's desk going through a pile of papers, a big, square-jawed man who looked like the executive he was. He rose as soon as he saw me and shook hands, saying, "I'm glad to see you, Garth. I've got a job for you and I hope you'll take it."

Ogle closed the door as Blake motioned me to sit down. He offered me a cigar, took one himself, and then sat down again in Ogle's swivel chair. He said, "You've worked off and on for the company as a shotgun guard for nearly two years."

I nodded, figuring he knew my record about as well as I did.

"You've worked in Deadwood as a policeman during the past two winters," he said. "I assume you know that we don't run as many stages in bad winter weather as we do most of the year, so we have less need for guards."

"I don't know as to that," I said. "I've always quit in the fall."

"Why?"

I hesitated, uncertain whether to tell him I preferred police work, thinking I had a better chance to hear about Jake Rawlins than I would sitting on the front boot beside the driver and holding a Winchester across my lap.

I finally decided not to tell him, so I said, "It gets pretty damned cold up there on the front boot. When I'm making my night rounds here in Deadwood, I can get warm once in a while."

"I realize I'm being nosy," Blake said, "but this job is a big one and I wanted to know a little more about you."

I sat there, not saying a word, still figuring it was his deal. When he saw I wasn't going to talk any more without some additional prompting, he said, "I'll lay it on the line, Garth. Your record has been an excellent one. I was just looking at it. No stage has been held up while you were riding it as a guard, although there were several attempts."

"That's right," I said.

He chewed on his cigar, then asked, "You can be released from your police job at any time?"

"That was my agreement," I said.

"Well, then, here it is," Blake said. "We are sending out a very large gold shipment in a treasure coach. The gold will be in a salamander bolted to the floor of the coach. We will send a large number of guards with the coach and we want you to serve as captain. The men will be experienced. They know and respect you, so I'm sure you won't have any trouble with them even though you'll be the youngest in the bunch."

Are you asking me if I'll take it?" I asked.

Blake nodded.

"Wages?"

"$200 to you," he answered, "and $100 to each of the other guards. We've never paid that kind of money before, but we think there is greater danger than usual on this trip."

He cleared his throat and glanced at Ogle, then brought his gaze back to me. "The truth is, Garth, we expect a determined effort on the part of an organized gang of road agents to rob this coach. We have a spy among them who sent us the information. The trouble is they have a spy in our organization, and they seem to know every move we make or plan."

Blake's face turned red with a sudden flare of temper. He added, "We'd done everything we can to root this bastard out, but so far we've failed. I suppose it's someone we trust and don't even suspect. By God, if I ever find out who he is, I'll kill him myself." He glanced at Ogle as if wondering if he might be the one, then brought his gaze back to me again. "How about it?"

"I'll take it."

"Good. We'll have one guard on the front boot with the driver and two on the rear boot. We'll have two more inside the coach. You and three others will be on horses acting as outriders. I have only two orders. One: don't scout so far from the coach that you won't be in position to help if it's attacked. Two: shoot to kill any armed stranger who approaches the coach."

I nodded agreement.

"The coach rolls out at four A.M. tomorrow. Be here. Don't tell anybody about it."

"I'll be here," I said, and rose.

Blake got up, too, and shook hands. "Do anything you need to do to get the coach to Cheyenne. You might just as well know the truth. This is the most important shipment we've ever made. The survival of the company depends on the job getting done. If we fail, we'll never be given another gold shipment. The miners will work together and hire their own crew to protect their gold and they'll ship it to Cheyenne themselves. They've made themselves plain on how they feel."

So that was the reason they had sent for me and the reason they were paying the money they were.

"We'll get it there," I said. I walked to the door and put my hand on the knob, then I turned back to face Blake.

"I've heard that the country as far west as the Powder River used to be crawling with road agents," I said. "I've likewise heard stories about famous outlaws like Jesse and Frank James hiding out somewhere in that country, Big Nose George Parrot and Sam Bass and others, but I had understood they'd drifted on because of the use of the treasure coach and the salamander and the use of extra guards. A few of them tried robbing the mail, but didn't make enough for it to be worthwhile."

Blake nodded. "That's true, but this is a new organization. I wasn't going to tell you, but since you brought it up, I will. A man named Jake Rawlins has combined several small bands of outlaws into one large outfit and promised them a big haul. From what I hear, this is the one they've planned all winter."

"I see," I said.

I left the office, not wanting Blake or Ogle to see my face. It might have told them too much. Maybe I was counting on this venture more than I should, but I had a feeling that I was going to pay my debt to my parents at last. Somewhere between Deadwood and Cheyenne I would kill Jake Rawlins.

I notified the police and went home. Daisy was irritated about me being late because she usually knew almost exactly when I would be home for breakfast and she always had it ready to eat. I told her what had happened and that mollified her, but it worried her, too.

"What is this treasure coach you mentioned?" she asked.

"The treasure coach is a specially built one," I answered. "It's designed to carry a valuable cargo. A man named Butler in Cheyenne makes them. The company has two. They're lined inside with steel plates five-sixteenths of an inch thick and they have port holes in the door that the men inside can shoot through."

"And the salamander?"

"It's a chilled-steel safe," I said. "Blake told me it would be bolted to the floor. Rawlins or any other outlaw will have a hell of a time getting the gold out of it even if they capture the coach which I don't think they can."

Daisy drew a long breath and shook her head. "Lane, when are you going to quit this kind of work?"

"Why should I?" I asked. "The pay's good."

"It's dangerous," she said. "That's why. Morg and I were talking about it last night. We want to get out of Deadwood. There's no future for any of us here. We want a horse ranch."

I laughed. "Morg would. He talks, eats, and sleeps horses."

"Why not?" Daisy demanded. "If we put our money together, we've got enough to buy a good horse outfit. Or start one from scratch if we find the right place. There's still good land to be taken if we get it now. If we wait, it'll all be gone the way people are swarming into this country."

She was dead right. I'd thought about it. As long as the Indians were a menace, this part of the country had not been settled except for the military posts and mining camps in the Black Hills, but now that the Indians did little more than make a nuisance of themselves by going on an occasional raid, the settlers were pouring in. Ranchers were driving in large herds of cattle and monopolizing the best range, so there wasn't going to be much left for the little fellows. The buffalo would soon be gone, leaving the grass for the cattle.

"You and Morg pick out a place?" I asked.

She shot me a questioning glance, suspecting me of hoorawing her, I thought. She shook her head. "No, not exactly. We did think about the Yellowstone Valley somewhere near Fort Keogh. The army buys lots of horses."

"Might be a good place," I said. "When I get back, we can go take a look at that country."

"Not unless Jake Rawlins is dead," she said bitterly. "Lane, you're possessed by that man. He's not worth it. Killing him won't bring your folks back."

I finished breakfast and rose, not wanting to argue with her or explain how I felt. I didn't think I could. I said, "I'm going to bed."

"Well, will it?" she demanded.

Her voice rose until it was almost a screech. We had been together almost two years, Daisy, Morg, and I,

135

and our relationship had been as near perfect as it could be. I mean, we got along well together, we never let our arguments get past the bantering stage, and each of us did our share of the work without complaint.

Daisy was seventeen and looked older, having filled out from the gangly, stringbean appearance she'd had the first time I saw her. She was a woman now, or close to it, and I'd been bothered by the fact that she wasn't meeting men who were or might be husband material. I hadn't pressed her, but if I mentioned anything about her finding a man, she'd get sarcastic or irritated, and toss her head and say, "Who needs a man?"

I felt guilty, I guess, keeping her here and not paying her anything. The fact that she was happy was beside the point, to my way of thinking. In a new country like this there was very little opportunity for a woman to make her own living by following a respectable profession, so getting married was about the only future she had.

Daisy had never used that high, angry tone on me before, and I didn't know what to say or do because I didn't think I'd done anything to bring on a tantrum. It was a side of her she had not shown me before, and suddenly I was angry. I had no intention of having a waspish-tempered girl on my hands.

I wasn't ready to give her an ultimatum, though, so I said, "No, it won't."

As I left the kitchen, I heard her say, "I'm sorry, Lane," and knew she was crying.

I slept until evening and got up and ate supper with Daisy and Morg, none of us saying anything about what I was heading into. I went back to bed for a few hours, then got up about three o'clock. As I shaved and dressed, I heard Daisy clattering around in the kitchen getting my breakfast.

"You didn't have to do this," I said when I went into the kitchen. "It's an ungodly hour to get up."

"I wanted to," she said. "I'll go back to bed after you leave. Morg said he would get his own breakfast."

As soon as I finished eating, I buckled my gun belt around my waist and, picking up my Winchester, started for the back door. Daisy was waiting for me. She put her arms around me and kissed me, and although she had kissed me many times, it had never been like this. Her lips were sweet and demanding, refusing to release mine for a good ten seconds, then she stepped back and looked up at me, tears in her eyes.

"You come back, Lane Garth," she whispered. "You hear me?"

I went on through the back door and crossed the yard to the small barn in the back where I kept Ginger. I lighted a lantern and saddled the horse, and all the time I was thinking uneasily, *that kiss had not been a sisterly one.*

CHAPTER XIV

When I reached the stage office it was nearly four. The coach was loaded and the horses were hooked up. The driver was sitting in his high seat, the lines in his hands. The other guards were there, bunched in front of the office door.

I reined up and dismounted. Several lanterns set on the platform gave a murky light to the scene that made it seem unreal. To me there was a strange, nightmarish quality about everything I saw here. Perhaps it was the smoky lantern light, or maybe the foreboding shadow of death that waited for us somewhere on the Cheyenne-Black Hills road. I knew it was not an unusual premonition, and that many soldiers had had it before battle during the Civil War.

Blake and Ogle were standing on the platform behind the lanterns. When Blake saw me step out of the saddle, he held up a hand for silence.

"You'll be rolling out in about five minutes," he said. "I want to remind you that this is the most impor-tant shipment we have ever made. I'm confident you men will get it through. If any of you have the slightest doubt, don't go."

He paused, and when no one said anything, or made a move to leave, he went on, "We have the fastest horses the company owns ready at every station to be hooked up the instant you arrive. We will change dri-vers, but you guards will go all the way to Cheyenne.

You will miss some meals. You'll stop for a few hours at Hat Creek station, but you won't get a full night's sleep. Garth will see to it that a guard is mounted while the coach is at Hat Creek. Any questions?"

No one asked anything, so he said, "You can expect to be held up and you can expect a fight, although there is a chance you'll go through without trouble. The shipment was scheduled to go out tomorrow morning. We moved it up one day hoping to fool the road agents, but if there has been a leak, they'll hear and be waiting for you." He motioned to me. "Garth, give them their positions."

Four company horses were saddled and waiting. I said, "I'll ride my horse." Blake nodded as if he understood. I distributed the men, telling Bud Jorgens, a veteran guard who had ridden with me several times, to take the scouting position in front with me.

I mounted, Jorgens selected his horse and stepped up, and the two guards I had tapped for the rear position swung into their saddles. I said to them, "Keep us in sight, but stay far enough behind so the road agents might not see you when they spring the trap. If you hear any shooting, come on the run." I touched Ginger with my spurs, saying, "Let's ride, Bud."

We trotted down Main Street. A moment later I yelled at the driver, "Roll 'em." I heard the silk crack with pistol-like sharpness in the still air, and the stage creaked and squealed as the driver angled away from the boardwalk and wheeled down the street about a block behind us.

A few minutes later we were out of Deadwood and had settled down for the long haul. The town lights disappeared, and the darkness was all around us, with no moon and only a few dim stars glittering in the cloud-laced sky.

Presently Jorgens asked, "What do you think, Lane?"

"I think we'll be lucky if we're still alive when we get to Cheyenne," I said.

"That's what I think," he said grimly. "How do you figure they'll hit us?"

"I don't have any idea," I said, "but I'm glad the road won't take us through Red Canyon the way it used to go."

"Hell, yes," Jorgens said. "They could pick us off from the rim." He was silent for a full minute, then he said, "I never heard of this man Rawlins. You know anything about him?"

"A little," I said. "He's a mean bastard."

"You know him?"

"Well, I've seen him," I said. "He used to be well known in New Mexico and Arizona. He ran with a gang that knocked over several banks."

"Is that so?" Jorgens said. "What happened to his outfit?"

"They were wiped out," I said. "All but him."

"It happens to all of 'em sooner or later," he said. "I guess Rawlins didn't have no trouble finding a new gang when he got up here."

"No, guess not," I said.

"Plenty of little bands of road agents," he said. "Hell, you could ride from here to Jackson Hole and pick up an army of 'em. Too bad we don't have somebody to organize a Vigilante Committee like they done in Virginia City."

Jorgens appeared to be talked out and we rode in silence most of the time after that. I thought of what he had said about a Vigilante Committee and I was glad we didn't have one. I guess the Vigilantes in Alder Gulch had done a good job and what they had done was necessary, but I didn't approve of them on general principles, mostly because I felt that it was another form of mob rule and because any real and lasting law and order had to come from a legitimate government.

It was full daylight before we reached Ten Mile. We had a five-minute stop while the horses were changed, then we were rolling again. Jorgens and I kept half a mile or more ahead of the coach, often dropping back if there was enough timber to hide the coach from us, or a long drop and climb into and out of a valley that was deep enough to make us lose sight of the coach.

We passed some traffic, and later in the morning we met the regular northbound coach. We waved, and the driver and guard waved back. We reined up and hipped around in our saddles to watch the coaches pass each other.

"Wonder if they'll guess what's in our coach?" Jorgens asked.

"Sure they will," I said. "The extra guards are a dead give-away."

"Yeah, I reckon so," Jorgens said as we rode on. "Seems to me it would be a good trick to send a treasure coach through with just one guard. The road agents would never figure out that it was carrying all that gold."

"They would if there's a leak in the Deadwood office," I said.

"I forgot about that," he said. "Who do you suppose it is?"

I looked at him, wondering if he was pulling my leg. I don't think he was. He was staring out across the sage-covered hills, only about half his mind on what he was saying.

"If Blake and Ogle don't know," I said, "there's not much way we could make an intelligent guess."

"It's a hell of a note when somebody you trust sells you out," he said. "How much dust do you suppose is in that salamander back there?"

"I don't have any idea," I said.

"I heard there was a quarter of a million dollars," he said.

I knew there could be that much, but I didn't say anything. Whatever the amount was, it had to be big for Blake and Ogle to take the precautions they were taking, and big for the road agents to tackle a party of guards the size of ours.

We went through Cold Spring, then Canon Spring, Beaver, and Jenney Stockade. I was vaguely disappointed, expecting the road agents to hit us sooner than this. I guess I was a little nervous by this time, wanting to get it over with. I considered the chance Blake had mentioned about going through without trouble to be a mighty slim one. There might, of course, be more than one attack before we reached Cheyenne, but I didn't expect it if we made their first attempt too costly.

Jorgens was getting jumpy, too. He wasn't saying much, but I could tell from the way he looked at me and then glanced quickly away, the corners of his mouth working. Once he said, "It's a good way to kill a man, just by letting him go on thinking he's gonna get killed."

"It's the waiting," I agreed.

We separated often, taking quick sashays into the hills on each side of the road. We topped the highest ridges to study the country ahead, but we never saw anything out of the ordinary. As the day dragged on, I began to wonder if we were going to be lucky and get through without trouble. I didn't believe it, but I sure as hell wanted to.

We crossed the Cheyenne river still without trouble, and my hope continued to grow that we had fooled the road agents. It was a foolish hope, and I think I knew it with the rational side of my mind. Presently the buildings of Burnt Creek station loomed ahead of us. I welcomed the prospect of getting my feet on the ground for a few minutes while the horses were being changed. I was thirsty, too, the day having been a warm one for spring.

When we reached the buildings, I said, "Ride around to your right, Bud. I'll go to the left."

No one showed up while we made our half circle. I thought that was strange. There was only a stock tender at the station, but it seemed natural that he'd come out of the stable or cabin to see who we were and what we were doing here. He had always been ready with the horses when any coach I'd been riding showed up. Still, I didn't think too much about it because this was not a scheduled coach and he might be taking a nap in the cabin. Or maybe he had just now remembered we were coming through and was in the stable frantically harnessing the horses.

When Jorgens and I met on the south side of the corral, Bud said, "Looks peaceful."

We turned back and reined up beside the big horse trough. I dismounted as the stage wheeled in, dust whipping up around it. The stock tender still had not appeared. I said to Jorgens, "You suppose the stock tender is asleep?"

"I'll bet he is," Jorgens said. "He has to get up twice in the night for the regular coaches. Chances are he takes a nap in the afternoon."

I stood beside the trough, letting Ginger drink. I was mighty damned uneasy all of a sudden, and I kept my eyes on the stable, prickles running up and down my spine. I should have got my hunch sooner, but I'd had nothing to go on except the one fact that the stock tender was not in sight.

"I'll go wake the old boy up," Jorgens said.

"No, stay where you are," I told him.

He looked at me, surprised. "What the hell?" he said. "You just going to let him sleep?"

"I don't know," I said. "All I know is something's wrong."

Johnny Trull, the guard who had been sitting beside the driver, had swung down and had moved the chock block so that it would block the coach's rear wheels. I felt Jorgens' eyes on me; he was scared and jumpy and confused by what I'd said.

"You don't think the bastards are in the stable?" he asked in a low tone.

"That's exactly what I think," I said.

A few seconds later it wasn't a matter of thinking. I knew.

A rifle barrel poked into sight between two logs of the stable wall. I saw the coach door begin to open. The guards inside were about to step out to stretch. "Stay inside," I shouted, and said to Jorgens, "Come on, Bud. We're sitting ducks out here."

I started toward the end of the stable on the run, expecting Jorgens to be right behind me, but he didn't move. I never knew why unless he was scared, or maybe thought he'd be worse off if he ran to the stable, being closer to the outlaws and therefore an easier target than if he stayed beside the trough. Anyhow, the next second a hail of bullets burst out of the side of the stable, one of them cutting Jorgens down, and another knocking Johnny Trull off his feet.

Of course there's no way of knowing how many bullets were aimed at me. I moved faster than I had ever moved in my life before, zig-zagging as much as I dared. I didn't want to take too much time to reach the stable. The firing was all coming from the far end. Once I reached the corner, they wouldn't see me.

I'm sure the plan was to kill all of us except the driver in that first burst of fire. He would be so busy holding the horses that he wouldn't be a threat to them. Although plenty of bullets were flying too close to me to be comfortable, I reached the stable without being hit; one bullet only ripped through the crown of my hat, and another one whipped through my shirt just below my left armpit.

For a moment I hugged the wall, panting hard. I heard the men inside the coach answering the road agents' fire, and suddenly it occurred to me that we might catch the outlaws in a crossfire if I could get around to the back side of the stable. I knew there was a door on that wall. We could bottle them up inside, I told myself, and wished Bud Jorgens had come with me like I'd told him.

I pulled my gun, and as soon as I had my breath back, I lunged around the back corner of the stable. The next instant I came as close to being killed as I had ever been. I didn't know they had a man guarding the door on the back side. In fact, I hadn't expected it because I thought they would use every gun they had to wipe us out before we knew they were in the stable.

The man was there, though, standing about five feet from the door. The instant I rounded the corner, he pitched a shot at me. My luck was still running high and he missed. He was so close to me that he should have hit me dead center, but the sun was behind me and he was looking directly at it. He must have been blinded. In any case he didn't have another chance. I shot him in the chest, the heavy slug slamming him hack and down as suddenly and violently as if an invisible rope had caught him and yanked him off his feet.

The sounds of firing from the other side of the stable was ear-shattering. I don't believe the men inside the stable could have heard the two shots behind it. Or if they did, they must have thought their man had knocked me out of the fight.

They knew, of course, that only one of us had reached the stable, and it would have been natural for them to assume their man had taken care of me, but it was an oversight that cost two of them their lives. The back door was open. I simply stepped into the doorway and gunned two of them down before the rest of them knew I was taking chips in the game.

Three of them wheeled and fired at me, but I jumped to one side in time, having expected this. I had no intention of lingering there in plain sight and furnishing them a clear target. I leaned my back against the wall and thumbed new loads into the cylinder, then waited, not sure what my next move should be now that they were aware I was here. I couldn't, of course, surprise them again. I didn't know how many were inside, but from the amount of firing I judged four or five of them were still alive.

I didn't wait long. For some reason the men inside panicked. I guess the reason wasn't too hard to guess, with three of the seven knocked off their feet in a matter of seconds. The firing from the coach hadn't slacked off, and the two guards riding in the rear would be coming in on the run to get into the fight.

The men inside must have had their horses in the stalls, saddled and ready to ride. I hadn't seen them in the brief time I had stood in the doorway, but I had had no time to look at horses. Now they came barreling out of the doorway like an avalanche roaring down a mountain side. I was hugging the back wall, but if I had been standing in the doorway they'd have run me down.

I was surprised, expecting them to fight it out to a finish. If they had, we would have paid a high price before we rooted them out. I was glad we didn't have to, though for a few seconds I thought I was a dead man. They were throwing lead at me from the time they cleared the door. None of the bullets hit me or even came close. I knew from experience it was very hard to hit a target from the back of a running horse.

Still, their bullets did dig up a lot of dirt around me. By the time I got untracked enough to start shooting, they were bent low in their saddles and moving hell-for-leather across the prairie. I emptied my gun at them, but I doubt that I hit any of them.

When they were out of range, I rose and reloaded, then circled back around the stable and yelled at the men in the coach to cease firing. I knew one thing for sure and it bothered me. I'd had a good look at the four men who got away, and I knew Jake Rawlins was not among them. The reason it bothered me was that I was reasonably sure that the men I'd killed did not include Rawlins, either.

I would never forget the strange, ape-like build of the man. The scar on his face might change his looks, but nothing could ever change the grotesque shape of his body.

The two rear guards had arrived now and dismounted. As soon as the men in the coach stepped out, I knew it was safe to take a look at the men I'd shot. I ran along the stable wall and opened the door on that side. The two men lay on their backs in the litter. Neither was Rawlins. He was still alive. Apparently he hadn't even been here with the road agents.

I stood there a long time before the other guards joined me. I was not likely to get a chance at Rawlins after all. I couldn't understand it. If this holdup had been planned by him, and if he had put this outfit together, he should have been here with these men. I couldn't make any kind of intelligent guess why he hadn't been.

CHAPTER XV

We found that Johnny Trull, the guard who had been on the front boot with the driver, was dead. Bud Jorgens had a leg wound that was paining him and bleeding enough to worry us. The first thing we did was to bandage the wound and stop the bleeding as much as we could. Then we loaded him into a wagon, hitched up a team, and, with one of the men who had been riding rear guard driving, we started him back up the road to Jenney Stockade. The wife of the man who ran the station wasn't a doctor, but she was the next thing to it, and I knew she'd do as much for Bud as anyone else short of Deadwood.

The stock tender wasn't anywhere around the station. We decided he must have been killed and the body hidden by the road agents. We carried Johnny Trull's body inside the cabin and left the road agents' bodies inside the stable. We hitched up six fresh horses and were on the road within an hour.

We traveled without a rear guard as far as Hat Creek station. I told the other man who had been riding behind the coach to take Trull's place on the front boot. I rode in front by myself. There was some danger of a second attack, but I refused to worry about it even though we were three men short.

I had no idea where Jake Rawlins was or where he had been during the fight, but it didn't seem logical that he'd have a second gang waiting farther south to hit us again. It seemed even less logical that another band would know about the coach and make a try for the gold.

If this had been the summer before, when the country west of the road seemed to spew road agents out of the ground and stage coaches were held up two or three times before they reached Cheyenne, I would have worried about being hit a second time, but a concerted effort on the part of various law enforcement agencies had almost cleaned the outlaws out.

Whether Rawlins had combined the few bands that remained to make up the gang that attacked us, or whether he had brought new men in was a question in my mind. Either way, I just couldn't believe we would be held up a second time.

My judgment was confirmed by the fact that we had no more trouble. We picked up another man at the Hat Creek station who rode rear guard all the way to Cheyenne. With that exception, there were no further changes in the crew.

All of us were dead tired when we reached Cheyenne. I had to stay in the office long enough to make a full report of what had happened, then I went to Dyer's Hotel, got a room, pulled off my boots, and fell asleep with my clothes on.

I had never been so tired in my life, partly because of the long hours in the saddle and being short of sleep, but mostly, I think, from the tension which had tied my nerves into a knot. There had been too much responsibility involved in getting all that gold to Cheyenne. I slept the clock around, woke up and went downstairs to the dining room and ordered the biggest steak they had, took a bath, and went back to bed shortly after noon.

That time I slept eight hours. I was still going strong when a knock on my door got me out of bed. It was black dark, so I had to fumble around on the bureau until I found a match. I struck it and lighted a lamp, then pulled on my pants and opened the door.

Two men stood in the hall, the light from a bracket wall lamp falling on their faces. One was a stranger; the other was a man I had met a number of times in Cheyenne and Deadwood, Special Agent John Murphy of the Post Office Department. He had been assigned this area more than a year before when some of the road agents, not satisfied with taking strong-boxes, had started pilfering the mail.

"Sorry to wake you up, Garth," Murphy said as he shook hands with me, "but we've got a job to do, and I didn't think we could afford to wait any longer." He motioned to the other man. "Garth, meet Deputy United States Marshal Al Keeber."

I shook hands with Keeber, thinking that something important was in the air or Murphy and Keeber wouldn't be working together, which I judged to be the case. I said, "Come in. I'll finish dressing while you talk."

"We'll wait downstairs in the lobby," Murphy said. "Come down as soon as you're dressed and I'll buy you another steak. I hear you had one at noon."

"What time is it?" I asked.

"About nine," Murphy answered. "We've got a night of riding ahead of us."

I groaned. "I've had enough riding for a while."

Murphy was a tall, thin-faced man with a very sharp nose and an equally sharp jutting chin that gave his face a hatchet-like appearance. His lips were thin so that his mouth looked like a narrow slit across the bottom of his smooth-shaven face. I had always considered him a humorless man, but now he laughed.

"I'll bet you have," he said. "I wouldn't blame you if you decided you wanted no part of this job. You certainly don't have to take it, but I'm going to give you the chance to turn it down."

"I'll be down in about ten minutes," I said.

I shaved and finished dressing and went downstairs. They rose when I entered the lobby, Murphy saying, "I already ordered the steak for you."

"We ate a couple of hours ago," Keeber said. "We'll just have a cup of coffee."

He was about as opposite from Murphy as a man could be, a full head shorter, round-faced, and heavyset without an ounce of fat on his stocky body. He reminded me of an undersized bull, but his size wasn't important. I instinctively felt that here was a man who would hold up his end of a fight, a feeling that's important when you're asking for trouble. If I read the signs correctly, that was exactly what we were going to do.

As soon as we sat down at a table, Murphy said, "You did a hell of a good job up there at Burnt Ranch station." He paused, then added, "With one exception."

I immediately bristled and had to bite my tongue to keep from snapping at him. After all, I was the man who had shot the outlaw guarding the back door of the stable, and I'd risked my hide by showing up in the doorway a few seconds later and knocking over two more men. I didn't like the idea of a man who hadn't even been there talking about exceptions.

I counted to ten mentally. Keeber seemed a little more perceptive than Murphy, or maybe the special agent didn't give a damn about my feelings. I'd heard he was sometimes a heartless, even cruel man. From his record, I could believe he was both.

"You overlooked one thing," Keeber said gently, "which same any of us might have done in the excitement of the moment and the necessity of getting on the road again."

Murphy nodded. "Did you notice that the stable had a hay mow?"

I shook my head. I hadn't thought there was a mow because the stable had a low roof and there simply wasn't enough room for much hay. Thinking about it now, I remembered noticing a shelf that ran the length of the stable over the horses. I hadn't climbed up to look, but I hadn't seen any hay up there, either. I did remember a stack back of the stable and I knew the stock tender had been feeding from it.

"It's not much of a mow," Murphy conceded, "and whoever built the stable was stupid because if he'd built the roof a few feet higher a lot more hay could have been stored there. I suppose the idea was to have just enough room for half a ton or so to use when blizzards hit. Anyhow, it's big enough for two men to hide up there."

"The stock tender," I said.

Murphy nodded. "And Jake Rawlins."

I sat there and stared at Murphy, my stomach rolling. I had been that close to him, a matter of a few feet, and I hadn't known or guessed he was there. I had missed him by an hour in Deadwood; this time by ten or fifteen feet. After almost five years of trying to catch up with the bastard, missing these two chances was just about more than I could bear.

My steak came along with hot biscuits and gravy and potatoes and coffee, but my appetite was gone. I asked, "Why was he up there?"

"Nobody knows," Murphy said. "Not for sure. The stock tender was with him, his hands and feet tied. Rawlins promised him that if he sneezed or coughed or breathed loud enough for anyone to hear he'd kill him on the spot. I'm not sure why they didn't kill him anyhow because that bunch are killers. I identified the men you shot. They were all wanted men with records of being killers. Rawlins rode off and left the stock tender tied. He got himself loose just before I rode in."

"Tell him where you were and what Ogle and Blake found out," Keeber said.

"Yeah, I'd better bring you up to date," Murphy said. "I was in Deadwood when you left with the treasure coach. You probably didn't know it, but the coach was carrying some registered mail along with the gold. That's why the Post Office Department is taking chips in this game." He shrugged. "Along with the fact that I'm still trying to clean out the road agents who have raised so much hell on the Cheyenne-Black Hills road the last year or so."

"I was here in Cheyenne all the time," Keeber said, "so I'm not tired, but John," he nodded at Murphy, "has had as much riding as you've had."

"I started south a few hours after the coach rolled out," Murphy went on. "I talked to Blake and Ogle just before I left. You know a man named Charley Offut who works for Ogle?"

I nodded. "A little mousy fellow with ink on his fingers all the time. I don't think I ever saw him when his fingers were clean."

Murphy nodded. "That's the man. He's the one who tipped Rawlins and his men off about the treasure. They were in Deadwood the night you barely missed Rawlins. They'd come in to talk to Offut. I understood you've been looking for Rawlins."

"That's right," I said.

"Well, Offut being the mousy kind of man he is," Murphy said, "Ogle never suspected him. He'd worked for the company for years, here in Cheyenne and then in Deadwood. Ogle says he would have banked on Offut being honest. When he found out the time for the treasure coach to leave Deadwood had been changed, he got a horse and rode out to where Rawlins was camped south of town. He was late getting to work the morning the coach left, and very nervous after he did show up. Ogle got suspicious and broke him down."

I had been toying with my steak, but I finally was

able to swallow it. The waitress came with a slab of dried apple pie and refilled my cup of coffee. I asked Murphy, "What's our job?"

"To find Rawlins," he answered. "Offut came out with the whole story. He'd been promised $10,000 of the loot, though it's my guess Rawlins never intended to pay it. Anyhow, he told Ogle that Rawlins and his outfit had been hiding out in the breaks west of Hat Creek station. Offut claims they'll go back there and wait till they've got a chance to try again.

"There's a little one-man cattle spread back there run by an old-timer named Royal. Offut says the outlaws just moved in with him without asking permission. They liked that spot because of its position, and because there's plenty of water and it's a hell of a rough country to get into. It's a good hideout.

"I know where it is. I've been there and stayed overnight with Royal. That's where we're going. Now you may think that three of us can't do the job, but it's my opinion that us three, being the men we are, can handle the job better than a big posse who likely would scare the whole bunch clear over to the Powder River."

"I'll agree to that," I said.

"Oh, I forgot to finish the part about Rawlins being up there in the mow," Murphy said. "The stock tender said Rawlins knocked some chinking out between the two top logs and was firing with the men downstairs. The stock tender said there was some idea about Rawlins shooting down into the coach from above and killing the guards who were riding inside the coach. You'll remember they didn't put armor on the top of the coach because of the weight.

"If the coach had pulled in close to the stable, the idea might have worked. Rawlins rode out as soon as the coach left. The rest of his gang were an hour ahead of him, but it's my opinion that Offut's right. They'll get together at Royal's place. Whether they'll stay and wait for another treasure coach is something else. They waited quite a while for this one. Men like that are pretty restless. The point is we'd better get started."

"I'll be ready," I said, "as soon as I go upstairs and get my hat and coat and gun."

Within the hour we were riding north. Twice I had come very close to catching up with Rawlins and missed. I had no real faith I'd do any better this time.

CHAPTER XVI

We left Hat Creek station at night, traveling west across the prairie. I didn't know the country. Al Keeber didn't, either, so our lives were in John Murphy's hands. He had said very little since we'd left Cheyenne, but just riding with a man gives you some idea of his caliber.

I instinctively liked Al Keeber, and I instinctively disliked Murphy, but I could not pinpoint the reasons for my feelings beyond the obvious fact that Murphy was a dour and silent man. I never knew what he was thinking except that he was hellbent on wiping out the rest of the Rawlins gang. I may be doing him an injustice, but I doubt that he thought very much about the cost to us, although I'm sure he didn't want to get killed.

I was convinced by this time that what I had heard about Murphy being heartless and cruel was correct. Still, I had no real evidence to support this belief except that he drove us hard, saying he was afraid we had already wasted too much time.

The sky was clear, with an impressive array of stars and a very thin moon, so there was some light to travel by. I thought Murphy rode too fast, but Keeber and I managed to keep up. Presently we came into broken country and Murphy was forced to slow up.

We crossed a small stream which I took for the headwaters of Old Woman Creek. We dropped into one ravine after another, then climbed out, most of the slopes being steep enough to make our horses labor. A cold wind sprang up, driving hard at us, so we rode with our heads down, our coat collars turned up around our necks. Then, an hour or so before dawn, Murphy reined up in the bottom of a steep-walled ravine.

"We'll stop here till daylight," he said. "We're almost there."

We pulled in close to a cutbank. We built a small fire and huddled over it. There was some timber here, and I wondered if there was enough timber around Royal's ranch to give us cover. Murphy lay down and went to sleep, though neither Keeber or I tried. He was a cold son-of-a-bitch, I thought, and I had a hunch we would not be taking any prisoners to Cheyenne for trial.

Murphy had scared the everlasting hell out of the road agents who had brought about what had been close to a reign of terror on the Cheyenne-Black Hills road the year before. He had shot and killed several. Others had left the country, so his idea of not fooling with arrests and trials may have done the job.

I felt the same way about Jake Rawlins, but I had a personal reason for hating him, whereas Murphy didn't know any of the outlaws we expected to find at Royal's ranch. I think he was one of those men who simply hated all law-breakers and didn't think they deserved a trial: the only thing they deserved was a slug in the brisket or a rope around the neck, and he acted accordingly.

He woke before the sun was up, and said, "We'll ride now." We did, Murphy leading the way out of the brush-choked ravine and across a ridge and down into another ravine. He stopped when we reached the bottom and said, "We'll leave the horses here."

By the time we had climbed to the top of the next hill, the sun was coming into view, its blinding light showing all along the horizon. Murphy said, "Stay down. I don't suppose any of 'em are out of bed yet, but we won't take any chances."

We lay flat on our bellies looking down on Royal's ranch. The cabin was a tight log structure. I saw several corrals and a log stable between us and the cabin, with a willow-lined stream running beside them. The light wasn't good enough to count the horses in the corrals, but there must have been eight or nine.

"Al, you stay here," Murphy said. "Give Garth and me about fifteen minutes. We'll work down the hill to the far corral. When I wave my hat, open up on the cabin. I don't care if you hit anything except the building. Garth and me will take care of 'em. I figure they'll swarm out of the cabin like rats running for shelter. Just one thing. Don't shoot Royal. You'll know him if you see him. He's big and old with a white beard and white hair. Ready, Garth?"

"Ready," I said.

I think we took more than fifteen minutes to reach the first corral because we angled back and forth to take advantage of every brush clump and boulder that we could find on the way down. I guess Keeber was able to follow us, all right, because he held his fire until Murphy waved his hat. We dropped flat on our bellies and waited. A few seconds later Keeber opened up.

A man had stepped out of the cabin and started to relieve himself when Keeber began to shoot. The fellow jumped about three feet and dove back through the door. Keeber worked his Winchester so fast they must have thought a dozen men were on that ridge top. He shot out the window, he put a couple of bullet holes in the stove pipe, and he must have drilled three or four through the open door.

As soon as he stopped shooting, two of them broke

out of the cabin and headed for the stable on a dead run. Murphy knew them better than I did. I guess they couldn't think of anything except getting to their horses.

"Now," Murphy said, and we opened up.

Neither man made it to the stable. Murphy knocked the first one down, and I got the second. Murphy's man struggled to his hands and knees and started crawling toward the stable. Murphy shot him again and this time he fell forward on his face and didn't move. I think the one I shot must have been dead by the time he hit the ground.

I dropped my Winchester and had started sprinting toward the cabin by the time Murphy finished his man. He yelled, "Hold it, Garth! Don't be a fool." But I guess I was a fool and I wasn't of a mind to hold anything. All I knew was that neither of the men we had shot was Rawlins, so Rawlins must be inside the cabin.

Maybe it wasn't very good reasoning, and maybe I was a fool for heading toward the cabin the way I did, but all I could think of was the seemingly obvious fact: Rawlins had to be in the cabin and my pursuit was over at last.

Of course Murphy had never intended to rush the cabin, not knowing how many men were inside, but I guess he thought he had to follow me. I kept my eyes on the open door and the shattered window in the front wall of the cabin, but no faces appeared. I charged through the door, my cocked gun in my hand.

Someone yelled, "Look out!" I guess it was old man Royal, standing behind me. Anyway, the next second a gun went off and a slug ripped into the wall beside me.

One man lay on a bunk in the far corner, a second man stood near the foot of the bunk, a smoking .45 in his hand. I fired before he could get off a second shot, the slug knocking him off his feet. He spilled backwards across the bunk and rolled off on to the floor.

The man on the bunk had his hands in the air, squalling, "I surrender. Don't shoot. I'm wounded." Murphy was only a few feet behind me. He shot the man on the bunk, killing him instantly.

"What'd you do that for?" I shouted at Murphy. "He was trying to give up."

"You can't trust these bastards," Murphy said. "Chances are he had a gun under his blanket just waiting for us to turn our backs."

"His hands were in the air." I was still yelling, thinking that all I'd heard of Murphy about not taking any prisoners was true. "He wasn't armed."

"Maybe," Murphy said. "Maybe not."

He crossed the room to the bunk and threw back the blanket. I followed him and, looking past him, saw the gun on the edge of the bunk. It was just about even with the dead man's belt buckle. He could have waited, as Murphy had said, until we turned our backs on him and then killed both of us with no risk to himself.

"I'll be damned," I said.

Murphy gave me a wry smile. "I've been over this ground before, Garth. Never trust 'em with nothing. Dead road agents don't hold up any more stages, neither." He wheeled to face Royal "Which one of these carcasses belongs to Rawlins?"

I turned to look at the old man. He was scared, so scared that his voice quavered when he said, "I told 'em you'd be along, Murphy. I knowed you would."

"Which carcass is Rawlins?" Murphy demanded.

"None of 'em," Royal answered. "I dunno where he is. After they got back from trying for the gold at Burnt Ranch station, they had a big row. All of 'em that got back was so sore at Rawlins they couldn't stand it. They blamed him for not getting the job done. He'd promised 'em the moon. He said there was no use staying here. He wanted 'em to go to Montana with him, but they wouldn't do it. Finally he just rode out and the rest stayed here. They figured to leave today."

"You gave these outlaws a place to stay," Murphy said. "Next time you'd better get word to us or I'll hang you along with 'em."

"Damn it, Murphy," the old man screeched. "I couldn't help it. I was a prisoner. I didn't let 'em stay. They just moved in."

"Remember what I said," Murphy snapped. "Find a way to get word to us next time." He jerked his head at me. "Let's get back to Keeber."

I left the cabin with him. I said, "We've got to help bury these men."

"That's Royal's business." Murphy glanced

164

obliquely at me. "You were a damned fool for rushing the cabin. If those bastards inside had been worth two cents, they'd have cut you down before you got to the door." He strode on, not looking at me again, then added a little grudgingly, "You're damned handy with your iron."

That, I thought, was about as great a compliment as Murphy could pay any man.

I picked up my Winchester and climbed the ridge to where Keeber was waiting for us. He asked, "How many?"

"Four," Murphy answered.

Apparently Keeber had no interest in how we'd done the job or who they were or anything else. I guess he figured it was done or we wouldn't be here and that was what counted.

I didn't say a word until we got to our horses and had mounted. Murphy and Keeber started back the way we had come, but I reined Ginger around and headed for Royal's place. Murphy yelled, "Garth, what the hell do you think you're doing?"

I pulled up and looked back at him. Keeber had stopped, too, and was staring at me. My dislike for Murphy boiled up in me and I said, "Murphy, I don't like your style. I'm going back to Royal's place and help him bury those men."

He snorted in contempt and touched up his horse and rode on in the direction he had started. Keeber hesitated, looked at me, then shrugged and followed Murphy.

By the time I reached Royal's place, he had hooked up a team to a wagon and loaded into it the two men who had been killed inside the cabin. He was surprised to see me, and more surprised, I guess, when I said, "I'll help you bury these men."

He looked at me, blinking, then he said, his voice still quavery, "I'd be obliged. Grave-digging is hard work for an old man like me." He took a long breath, then added, "That Murphy is a hard man."

It took us the best part of the day to dig the graves on the hillside above Royal's cabin. When we finished, he said, "Stay the night, Garth. I'll go fix some supper."

I didn't need a second invitation. I was hungry and tired and sleepy. Royal hadn't said much all day, but he talked some while we ate. He was a lonely old man who had suffered at the hands of various outlaw bands, but he didn't want to move. He told me he was the one who had sent word to Blake about what the road agents had planned.

He didn't like people and he hated what he called civilization because, he said, it just wasn't civilized. He finally admitted the outlaws had paid him for putting them up, so it looked as if he was playing both ends against the middle. I thought that if Murphy knew that, he'd take the old man in, but I had no intention of doing anything about it.

By the time we finished supper, I was almost asleep in my chair, but I had to ask one question. "Where do you think Rawlins would go in Montana?"

"I dunno," Royal said. "He talked some about Miles City, though I dunno why he'd want to go there. Ain't much of a burg, from what I hear."

I slept until sunup and Royal cooked a mess of flapjacks for me. Before I left, I said, "Try thinking about it again. Did Rawlins give you any idea where he might go besides Miles City?"

He shook his head. "I've been thinking about it ever since you asked last night. It's a big, empty country up there in Montany. Worse'n Wyomin', I reckon. He could go anywhere and get swallowed up." He squinted at me for a moment, then he said, "I dunno why you'd ever want to find that ugly bastard. He's about the meanest son of a bitch I ever did see."

"I want to find him to kill him," I said, and rode away.

I took my time getting back to Deadwood. I was drained dry. Somehow my life seemed futile, almost unreal, as if I was destined to spend it looking for Rawlins and never catch up with him. When I reached Deadwood and was putting Ginger away in the barn, Daisy heard me and came running out of the house.

"Lane," she screamed. "Lane, I'm so glad you're back."

She hugged me and kissed me and cried for a while. We went into the house, our arms around each other. My life didn't seem so futile then, and it came to me that if a man is loved by someone else, it can't be completely empty.

When Morg got in that evening, he was almost as

happy to see me as Daisy had been. He pumped my hand and slapped me on the back and said he was sure glad I was home again and all in one piece.

"The way I hear it," he said, "there's been a few bullets flying around where you were. I kept asking in the office about you. I guess Murphy sent a report in, so we all figured you were alive and kicking."

We had one of Daisy's good suppers, then I told them how it had been, leaving out only one pertinent fact. I didn't tell them that Royal had said Rawlins was headed for Montana and maybe Miles City. Instead, I said, "I've been thinking about this notion of having a horse ranch. I guess we'd better go to Montana and see what we can find."

I couldn't have pleased them more. Morg shook my hand again and Daisy kissed me again, and I felt like a hypocrite for not telling them that Montana was a good place to look for Rawlins. I told Daisy she had to stay right where she was because I'd heard that Miles City was no place for a decent woman if she aimed to stay in a hotel. We'd send for her, I said, as soon as we found a place to live. She didn't like it, but finally promised to do what I told her.

Three days later Morg and I were riding toward Miles City.

CHAPTER XVII

Miles City was located on Tongue River just above its junction with the Yellowstone. I hadn't been in town more than an hour before I saw that it wasn't much of a town, but it was tough, tougher, I thought, than Dodge City.

I was glad I had told Daisy to stay in Deadwood until I sent for her. There simply were no decent hotel accommodations. Most of the buildings were frame with false fronts and were scattered haphazardly along Main Street, which was the road that came in from Bismarck and went on across the Tongue River to Fort Keogh two miles beyond. I didn't need more than a few minutes to see that the great percentage of these buildings were either saloons or whorehouses.

Fort Keogh had been built shortly after the battle of the Little Big Horn. The following winter General Miles had campaigned with his infantry against the hostiles who had refused to come in and become reservation Indians. How he had been able to operate at all with the temperature 40 degrees below zero is something I never understood, but he had done it, and brought in the Indians to boot.

The fort was still here. Its payroll, of course, was the biggest in the country and I suppose the businessmen depended on it. The soldiers were very much in evidence, a fact that did not elevate the town in either Morg's or my opinion. It was said among cowboys that when a whore got old and worn out, she went to the dogs, and then on down to the soldiers. This may have been something of an exaggeration, but it was about the attitude Morg and I had toward the soldiers.

One of the first things I learned was that Miles City was a great shipping point for buffalo hides and that during the previous winter thousands of buffalo had been killed along the Yellowstone, that the river bottom all the way down from the mouth of the Porcupine was sprinkled with the bones of buffalo that had been killed for their hides, the meat being completely wasted.

One of the first men I got acquainted with was Tuck Loman. He'd been in Montana Territory ever since they'd laid the chunk and he knew it, I think, better than anyone else in Miles City. He was a bald-headed man in his early fifties with a ragged beard and mustache, short, broad-shouldered, and as strong as a small bull.

I met him first in the Cottage saloon on the corner of Main and Park streets. He owned a livery stable located on Main about a block east of the Cottage, but he didn't pay much attention to it, just turned the running of it over to a young fellow named Charley Higgins. He owned a small spread up the Rosebud, but he didn't pay much attention to that, either. He let his foreman take care of it while he hunted or guided other hunters or played poker or just hung around the saloons and whorehouses.

Tuck was one of the few free spirits I ever met in my

life. If he'd lost his livery stable and ranch, he wouldn't have worried a bit. He'd have saddled up, bought a few necessities, and gone out and lived off the country. He'd have enjoyed doing it, too.

Maybe I cottoned to him because he was such a free spirit. Or maybe because he was a good storyteller. Or again maybe it was because he hated soldiers and hide hunters. Whatever the alchemy was, I felt that he was an old friend within a matter of minutes after I met him.

"By God," he said, "I've met some dirty sons-of-bitches who ain't took a bath since Heck was a pup, but the hide hunters just boggle your mind. They ain't human. They never bathe and they never change clothes, and you wouldn't believe how they stink." He scratched a stubble-covered cheek, and added thoughtfully, "I do believe they're worse than the soldiers."

Morg and I stayed three days in Miles City, camping in a grove of cottonwoods along the Tongue. I spent quite a bit of time with Tuck, partly because he was entertaining, but mostly because he knew the country and was willing to tell me what he knew.

Morg spent most of his time at the fort and found out what the army wanted in the way of horseflesh and about how many horses they'd take in a year. I don't know that he got any promises from the officer who did the buying, but at least he was assured he'd have his share of the army's business if he had the right horses.

When I mentioned to Tuck that we were looking for a ranch site, he said, "I'll tell you one thing, Lane. This is the time to grab what you want. I'll make you a standing bet that in less'n five years every decent place in Montana where you could start a ranch will be taken."

"I won't take that bet," I said. "I'd lose."

He grunted something and tongued his cigar to the other side of his mouth and kind of squinted at me, then he said, "Go buy yourself some grub and get your pack horse loaded up. I'll take you up the Tongue in the morning. If we don't find the kind of place you want, we'll try the Rosebud."

It was more than I had any right to ask. I said, "I'll pay you for your time . . ."

"You say that again and I'll shoot you dead," he said amiably. "Just get plenty of grub. I've been hanging around this burg until I'm sick of it. There ain't a woman in town or a bottle of whisky that interests me any more. I've got to get out into the big open and get me some fresh air."

I got hold of Morg and told him about it. We bought supplies and next morning loaded up our pack horse. Tuck rode in on a black gelding that started my heart to pounding the minute I saw him. He was my father's old horse, the same one I'd seen in Deadwood that told me Jake Rawlins was probably in the country.

"Where'd you get that horse?" I demanded.

He looked at me questioningly, not understanding why I suddenly took on the manners of a crazy man.

"Why, I bought him," he said. "Just a few days ago. He ain't been taken care of real good, but he's a fine animal. He's coming out of it in just the little time I've had him."

"Who'd you buy him from?"

"Why, I dunno," he answered. "Never gave his name. A big booger with a scarred-up face and a beard. You know, I seen a big ape once in a zoo. St. Louis, I think it was. Or maybe Chicago. I disremember. Anyhow, this gent reminded me of the ape. The way he was built, I guess, and his long arms. Looked and smelled like a hide hunter, but he claimed he'd been prospecting in the Black Hills."

"Where'd he go?"

Tuck shrugged. "I dunno that, neither. Rode north from here. I suppose he'll get a job cutting wood on the Missouri or Yellowstone for the steamboats, then wind up back here, come winter, and shoot bufflers. Long as they last, that is." He squinted his eyes at me again, and asked, "You know him?"

"Yeah, I know him," I said, and wondered how close I'd come to catching Rawlins in Miles City. "Why did he sell the horse?"

"Said he was short of money," Tuck answered. "After selling him to me, he showed up at the livery stable the next day with a roll of bills big enough to choke a black bull and bought another horse, younger and in better shape, and also a pack animal. Then he left town, but he never gave no hint where he was headed."

"Let's get moving," I said.

Afterwards Morg fell in beside me. He said sourly, "So now you know Rawlins has been in Miles City."

I nodded, and said, "I guess I knew it all the time. I likewise know he'll be back. All I've got to do is to stay here and wait."

Morg stared at me, his lips pulled tight against his teeth. He said in a low, angry tone, "Don't tell Daisy. She's mighty damned tired of hearing about Jake Rawlins. If she thinks you're gonna take off after him again, she won't stay."

"Jake Rawlins is my business," I said. "If Daisy wants to go somewhere else, I won't stop her."

"You wouldn't stop me, neither," he said, his lips still tight against his teeth. "I'm about as tired of you wasting your time chasing Rawlins as Daisy is. You ever gonna settle down and start living like a white man?"

About that time I was pretty damned hot under the collar. "Now you just look here, Morg," I said. "You live the way you want to live and I'll live the way I want to live. If trying to find Jake Rawlins is part of my way, then I aim to go right on chasing him."

"You don't figure you owe anything to Daisy?" he asked. "Or me?"

"No," I answered. "Why should I?"

"I ain't saying a word about me," he said, "but Daisy's in love with you. That ought to be enough to make you stay home and take care of her. Of yourself, too. She ain't a girl no more in case you ain't noticed. She's a woman."

Of course I'd noticed, but Morg was crazy when he said she was in love with me. Before I could tell him, he touched his horse with his spurs and caught up with Tuck. I thought about it some then. Sure, she loved me, but it was like a brother, not the kind of love Morg was talking about, and I loved her like a sister. It struck me that Morg was in love with her himself or he wouldn't be thinking and talking like he was. I wondered if he'd ever told her.

She was, of course, a lot closer to Morg's age than to mine. He was still a lot of boy, but he'd grown up into quite a man, too, not as tall as I was, but mighty well built in the shoulders and arms. He could handle himself and he could get a job anywhere they had horses. Daisy could do a lot worse. Maybe I ought to tell her.

He didn't say anything more about it. After we had supper that night and were sitting around the fire smoking and talking, Tuck got off on his experiences with the Vigilantes around Virginia City in the early days.

"It was a rough time, I tell you," he said. "Lots of folks look back nowadays and condemn the Vigilantes for doing what they done, but Plummer was the sheriff, so the law just wasn't doing anything. I don't know what would have happened if the Vigilantes hadn't done what they did. It was getting so nobody's life or property was safe. Maybe Vigilante law ain't a good thing, but it's better'n no law."

He threw his cigar stub into the fire and lighted another one. "If you're aiming to settle down here,

Lane, you'd better do some thinking along this line. We never have enough law officers in a country like this. Right now it ain't so bad, but it'll get worse. The steamboats will quit running when the railroad gets here, so they won't need wood-cutters no more. The buffler will be gone, so the hide hunters will be looking for work, only chances are they won't take the jobs they can get. Now what do you reckon all them tough hands will do?"

"Turn outlaw," I said.

"That's exactly what they'll do." Tuck jerked his cigar out of his mouth and jabbed it at me. "If the law don't hunt 'em down and hang 'em, and you'n me know the damned law won't, who's gonna stop 'em from robbing this country blind?"

"I don't know," I answered, "and I'll kill any bastard who comes around my place stealing my stock, but I don't want any part of a Vigilante Committee. The cure would be worse than the disease."

Tuck grinned, shrugged his massive shoulders, and put his cigar back into his mouth. "We'll see," he said. "I've known some real good men to change their minds."

I didn't argue with him. As a matter of fact, I never gave another thought to outlaws or a Vigilante Committee. I was thinking about Daisy and what Morg had said about her not being a child any more. Of course I had seen her develop and outgrow her child's body, but I knew, now that I thought about it, that I still thought of her as a child.

Then I started remembering the way she had kissed me when I'd left Deadwood to ride south with the treasure coach, and how we'd walked with our arms around each other after I got back. And I thought about how it had been having her keep house for us in Deadwood, keeping it clean and cooking the way she had and all.

I didn't want to marry her. I didn't want to marry any woman. A woman held you down and there were things you had to do and other things you couldn't do if you had a wife. I guess it was a sort of maternal slavery and I wasn't ready for it. Why? Well, that was a question I didn't like to face. The normal way of life for a man was to marry and have children and face the responsibility that came with marriage. I just wasn't ready to live a normal life.

Of course I knew why I didn't want to answer that question. I just didn't want to admit to myself what the answer was, but I had to. I lay there with my head on my saddle, the fire dying down, and stared at the black, star-studded sky, and finally told myself the truth. I'm not sure, but maybe it was the first time I had been completely honest with myself.

I was married to the proposition that I was going to kill Jake Rawlins and I was not going to let anything get in the way or stop me. I didn't have any place in my life for a wife. It would be a form of bigamy if I got married, and I guess this was what both Daisy and Morg were thinking.

After a long time I finally started to rationalize. I

told myself that Morg was wrong about Daisy being in love with me. Maybe he could talk her into marrying him and staying with us. I'd probably spend my winter in Miles City. That was where Rawlins would show up, and I intended to be there when he did, not way up the Tongue River on a horse ranch.

When I finally dropped off to sleep, I had come to only one conclusion. I didn't want to go back to Morg's cooking. He'd just have to do something to keep Daisy.

CHAPTER XVIII

We hadn't traveled more than five miles the next morning when we rode into a small basin that was practically covered with buffalo. Morg looked at me and I nodded and he reined away from the river toward them. In a few minutes he had a big bull down and I never saw a happier boy in my life.

Ordinarily Morg was not one to show much emotion, though I'd learned to tell when he was happy or moody or angry, but this time he let himself go, whooping and hollering and prancing around the dead bull as if he were crazy.

I hadn't realized how important it had been to him to kill a buffalo, although he had said several times with regret that he wished he'd killed one when we'd seen that small herd on our way north to Deadwood nearly two years ago. We both knew the buffalo wouldn't last much longer, and I guess that what had been eating at him was this knowledge that time for him to get one was running out.

Anyhow, he had what he wanted and we needed fresh meat, so we were all happy. We took the tongue and fries or mountain oysters and some tenderloin, knowing we couldn't keep all of it from spoiling. We rode on south, up and down countless steep-walled draws, most of them with dry bottoms, and now and then crossed a grassy valley, all the time keeping in mind what we were looking for.

On the afternoon of the third day we found it, a wider valley than most with fine grass and a bench east of the river with some sage and a good deal of grass, too. We could see plenty of yellow pine timber on the buttes beyond the bench. Long spurs ran from some of the buttes down to the bench and they, too, had a scattering of timber on them. There was also a good deal of black ash and box elder along the Tongue.

One important fact that struck me was the way the east bank of the river sloped down to the water. It was also true of the edges of the stream which flowed from the timber through the middle of the valley. Its sloping banks would give the cattle no difficulty getting to water.

I could foresee the time when land was scarce and all of the valleys we had seen since we had left Miles City would be settled, but the trouble with most of them was that the banks of the river and the tributaries were so steep that it would be difficult to cut them down to the point where stock could get to water. I was glad that Morg and Daisy had prodded me into looking for a ranch site when they had.

Several other things struck me, too. If feed became scarce, we could raise hay in the bottom. There was plenty of timber for building and fuel. The bench had enough sage to hold some of the snow so it wouldn't blow off and drift. Later in the year, when grass was gone from the bottom land, the bench would furnish good pasture.

"Well, Morg," I said, "we could hunt all summer, but I don't think we'll ever find a better spot than this."

"I don't, either," Morg said. "How about calling our spread the Big D?"

He didn't have to explain that it was his way of honoring Daisy. I'd had the idea we'd call it the LM for us, but now that he'd suggested the Big D I didn't intend to buck him on something that wasn't really important, so I nodded agreement.

"Where will we put the buildings?" I asked.

"I'd say yonder among them small pines." Morg nodded upstream. "If the water's any good, we could pipe it into the house. It'd save Daisy a lot of time."

"Good idea," I said.

We rode up the creek to the place he was talking about and camped there for two days, riding back and forth across the bench and into the timber and along the bank of the river. We picked the spot for our house just above our camp site, then staked out the positions for the stable and corrals downstream from the house.

"I'll ride back to town," I said, "and fetch out a load of supplies. We'll need a team and wagon. I'll bring a tent, too. Daisy can sleep in it till we get the house up."

"I'll stay here with Morg," Tuck said. "He might need some advice from an old hand. I've built a few log houses in my day. Maybe I'll be of some help."

"Sure you will," Morg said.

I nodded agreement, then asked, "You know of any good men we can hire? Looks to me like it's one hell of a big job starting a spread from scratch this way."

I was realizing now what a dreamer I'd been. When we'd bought the place up the Picketwire from Trinidad and later when I'd bought the ranch on the St. Vrain we'd had something to start with. Sure, they were both rundown, but it was easy enough to see what had to be done. Here we had nothing but the land, running water, and timber. What we did with those three basics was up to us.

Tuck just kind of laughed when I said that. I guess he considered us children who had bitten off a bigger chunk than we could chew. He said, "You're dead right, Lane. It's one hell of a big job. Go see Charley Higgins in my livery stable. He'll know who's working and who ain't. There's several good men around town you can get if they don't have jobs."

I started back to Miles City at dawn, telling Morg I'd get a letter off to Daisy. I made it to town in one day by riding hard. We'd taken all of two days and

181

part of a third to reach our future home, but we'd ridden slowly, looking at the country and thinking about what we wanted. This time there was nothing to hold me.

That night I wrote to Daisy, telling her when to be in Miles City and that I'd meet her because there wasn't a decent place for a woman to stay. I gave her two weeks, not knowing how long it would take for the letter to get to her, or how much time she'd need to sell off the furniture we had bought. I bargained with Higgins for a team, asked about men and hired two, then bought a wagon and the supplies we needed, and was on the road again in the morning, rolling south.

The men I hired beat me to our valley. When I wheeled in with the wagon, they were felling timber for our buildings. "Good men," Morg told me that night, and added, "but that Tuck Loman is one in a million. Looks to me like he knows all there is to know about this country. The Lord sure had His hand on your shoulder when you met up with Tuck."

"Fools rush in where angels fear to tread," I said. "I didn't know all we were up against when we left Deadwood."

"I've been thinking the same," Morg said. "Well, Tuck and me have made some plans. Soon as Daisy gets here and you can be home all the time, we're riding south to the Cheyennes and dickering for horses. Tuck says he's done it and they have some pretty good animals, better than the average Indian ponies."

"Probably stole them from the Crows," I said, "who

stole them from some white outfit that went through the country."

"Probably," he agreed, "but we don't need to think of that. Whoever lost 'em ain't gonna get 'em back from the Cheyennes."

"No, I don't think they will," I said. "About me staying home. I don't figure on being here all winter. I thought I'd stay till you're lined out, then I'll go into Miles City. They might need a good lawman."

He stared hard at me for several seconds, his face turning dark with anger, then he said, "Rawlins," making the word sound as if it were an oath.

Morg turned his back on me and walked away. I was plain sore about the way he and Daisy felt about my pursuit of Rawlins. They both should have had more understanding. I'd been after Rawlins long before I knew either one of them. They had no right to expect me to quit now.

I made two more trips into Miles City before I went to meet Daisy. I bought more supplies and had the wagon loaded by the time the stage rolled in from Deadwood. It hadn't been so long since I had seen Daisy, but somehow she looked different when she stepped down from the coach.

She was seventeen, almost eighteen, but I had been thinking of her as a girl just as I always had. Now I was sure that Morg had been right when he'd said she was a woman. Some girls mature early, some later. Daisy was an early one. It took these weeks of being away from her for me to see it.

Maybe it was the way she was dressed. She had bought some new clothes I hadn't seen before, a small blue hat that was tipped pertly on one side of her head, and a white shirtwaist and a dark green skirt that fitted her snugly at waist and breast.

I had lived in the same house with Daisy and Morg for nearly two years, but now, suddenly, I sensed a degree of womanliness in Daisy I had not felt before. In that moment I became uneasy, a crazy notion coming to me that I did not know her, that I was taking a stranger home to the Big D.

She ran to me when she saw me; she hugged and kissed me, then clung to me as if we had been apart for years instead of weeks. I was ashamed, for my clothes were not as clean as they should have been, I needed a haircut, and I hadn't shaved for a week. But Daisy wasn't bothered by my appearance, or at least didn't show it beyond saying, "You've missed having a woman around, Lane. I'll bet Morg has, too. Don't let it happen again. You need me."

I wasn't so sure of that as I carried her valises to the wagon and went back for her trunk. I set the trunk in the wagon bed beside her valises, gave her a hand up to the seat, and climbed in beside her. For some reason I felt ill at ease with her. I never had before. I didn't know why I felt that way. Perhaps it was because I was remembering what Morg had said about her being in love with me. Or maybe it was the simple fact that I realized what she expected of me and I knew what I still had to do, and that the two could not be reconciled.

We didn't say anything more until we were out of town and wheeling south up the Tongue, then Daisy said, "You were right about Miles City not being much of a town. I'm glad you were on hand to meet me."

"It'll be a good town in time," I said, "but it's like any brand new place in the West. It's pretty wild at first."

"Do you have our buildings up?" she asked.

"No, but we've got most of the logs cut and hauled," I answered. "It won't be long now. We have a tent for you to sleep in."

"Good," she said.

She sat very close to me on the wagon seat. We rode in silence for a time, then Daisy began telling me gossip about Deadwood and the stage line and the most recent holdups. Then tension was gone and I felt she was the same Daisy I had known in Deadwood. I decided the feeling had been imagination on my part, that Daisy hadn't changed at all.

We camped that night in a grove of black ash along the river. After we had eaten, we sat by the fire for a long time, Daisy hugging her knees with both arms. She hadn't mentioned Jake Rawlins. I hadn't, either, and I wasn't going to, knowing she would react the same way Morg had.

"It's a big, wild, beautiful country, Lane," she said dreamily. "We didn't meet anyone on the road all afternoon. You think it will always be this way?"

"No," I said. "It won't be this way much longer."

I told her about Morg killing the buffalo, and about his plan for trading with the Cheyennes for horses. I said, "You're going to be in for a lot of hard work. It's tougher getting a ranch built than I'd thought."

"I'm not afraid of hard work," she said. "Not when it's for the men I love."

"It's good to have a sister," I said.

She stiffened and turned her gaze on me. In the dusky light I saw her face turn pale and her mouth firm out the way it did when she was angry or unhappy. She said, "I am not your sister, Lane Garth. Maybe you feel that way about me, but it's not the way I feel about you."

We went to bed a short time later, Daisy not saying another word to me. The night was not a cold one, but some time before dawn I woke to find Daisy snuggling against me. When she saw I was awake, she whispered, "Hold me, Lane. I'm cold. Get me warm. Please."

I put an arm around her and drew her up close to me and pulled my saddle blanket over her. She was shivering. I didn't understand it because it just wasn't that cold. I said, "I'll build the fire up."

"No, just hold me," she said. "I'll get warm in a little while." She was silent, then she said, "Don't be mad at me, Lane."

"I'm not," I said.

"Don't let me be mad at you, either."

I didn't say anything to that, but it seemed an odd

request. I didn't see how I could keep her from being mad at me. That was up to her.

We started south again at sunup and reached our valley that evening. Morg ran to meet us and helped Daisy down from the wagon seat. She hugged and kissed him, but not the way she had hugged and kissed me. I had the notion as I watched her that Morg was a brother, but I wasn't.

We introduced the other men, Tuck saying, "Things are going to be better around here. At least we'll have some beauty in camp."

"And better cooking," I added.

Daisy wasn't listening. She stood looking around, at the creek and the bench above it and timbered buttes to the east and the river on the west; then she said, so softly I barely heard, "It's beautiful, just the way I had dreamed it would be. I'm going to live and die right here."

CHAPTER XIX

I thought I had worked hard before in my life, but I hadn't known what hard work was, nor long hours and short sleep. We were all driven, I think, by a compulsion to get the ranch in shape for winter, but there were more things to do than we had dreamed. I never once urged Daisy or Morg to get something done. They were always right up with me or ahead of me.

Tuck surprised me. Sometimes it seemed to me that he felt it was his ranch we were building, for he worked as long hours as we did and fully as hard. As a matter of fact, we couldn't have accomplished as much as we did without him because he had the savvy we lacked. More than once, particularly in building the house and stable and outbuildings, his advice saved us from having to do some jobs a second time.

Before the summer was over, I learned that this was his way. He simply was too bored to sit around town very long. He had a wife on his ranch on the Rosebud, and I guess that was one reason he worked so hard with us. He didn't want to spend any more time with her than he had to. Besides, he was crazy about Daisy.

"By God, that girl is one in a million," Tuck told me one evening after we left the supper table. "I wish I had a daughter like her." Then his face turned grave and he said with keen regret, "But I never will. I don't even hope no more."

We were lucky, too, in regard to the men I'd hired. I had considered them temporary help because they were older men than I wanted, but at the time I couldn't get anyone else. Both of them were ten years older than Tuck, maybe more. Al Leeper was a bachelor, Ed Kelsey a widower. Neither had any family, neither had any money saved, and both wanted work. I found they were dependable, they understood the country, they'd had some experience building log structures, and they knew stock.

By the time fall came, Morg and I felt we wouldn't do any better, so we offered them winter jobs at half pay. They jumped at the chance, Kelsey saying, "Anything's better'n hanging around Miles City's saloons begging drinks and meals."

As soon as the pressure of building let up, Morg and Tuck rode south and traded with the Cheyennes for thirty head of horses. He sold twenty of them to the army for a good profit, then he and Tuck went to work breaking the other ten.

I heard about a little cow outfit on the Powder River that wanted to sell some cattle, so I took Al and Ed and rode over there. The cows weren't the best, but I didn't know where I'd find better stock. I'd try to pick up a few good bulls later on, I thought, probably some Durhams that had been brought in from Oregon. We drove our small herd home, threw them on the bench, and cut all the hay we could from the bottom land.

"Ranchers here don't put up much hay," Al Leeper said. "Most winters you don't have any need for it. This is like the rest of the plains country, the short grass makes good feed all winter, but once in a blue moon you get a son-of-a-bitch of a winter. With so much snow, the cattle can't get at the grass. Then you'll wish you had some hay. They'll all come to it. You'll see."

Leeper was a lanky, tobacco-chewing man who had been a trapper in his younger days. He'd been all over the Rockies and on out to the Pacific coast. He'd made half a dozen small fortunes, the biggest when he'd hit the jackpot in Virginia City, and he'd lost them all. He wasn't a man who could manage anything of his own, but as long as he was told what to do by someone else, he was a good worker.

"I've seen a lot of men like him," Tuck told me one day. "As long as they're able to work, they'll get along, but what are they gonna do when they're too old to earn wages?"

I didn't know and I didn't try to answer Tuck, but the same question had occurred to me. We took care of old horses who weren't worth their keep any more, but we seldom took care of old men. There wasn't much I could do about it except make sure I didn't wind up the same way.

Our house worked out fine, four rooms, tight and solid and bigger than the place we'd rented in Deadwood. I hauled shingles and flooring and windows and doors from Miles City, and then the furniture we needed. I didn't try to hold back, but bought the best I could, figuring that was the better bargain in the long run.

We had thrown all our money into a common pot. Morg had the least. He was touchy about it, saying it wasn't fair to Daisy and me to cut him in as a full partner, but Daisy and I outvoted him. I had considered it carefully, knowing we were doing more for him than he had any right to expect; but I also knew that when I left the Big D to winter in Miles City, it would be up to Morg to take hold and run the outfit.

I was being selfish and maybe not quite fair, but I wanted Morg to have a big enough interest in the spread to make it worthwhile for him. I didn't tell

Daisy how my thinking ran, and I don't know that she thought of it at all, but it was her idea to make Morg an equal partner as much as it was mine.

By the time we had everything shaped up with a winter's supplies in the cellar, our capital was running pretty low. We had built a log bunkhouse not far from the house. Leeper and Kelsey slept in it, and Tuck too, as long as he stayed with us.

We ate in the kitchen. Daisy cooked for all six of us, and not once even when we were working the hardest during the hot summer months did she complain. Night after night I knew she was dead tired, but she could always smile and say it wouldn't be so bad next winter. She'd catch up on her sleep then.

We built a dam in the creek just above the house and had a pond of clear, cold water that was shoulder-deep. It was one of the things most responsible for getting us through the summer when we'd worked in the hot sun all day.

Morg and Daisy and I swam every night before we went to bed. It was our way of bathing along with having a few minutes of fun. Come winter, we'd do our bathing in the kitchen as we had done in Deadwood, but as long as the days were hot, the pond served very well for us.

Late in September Tuck told me he had to leave us. He said, very honestly I thought, that he had enjoyed the summer and hoped we made a fortune out of the Big D. When I tried to pay him, he acted insulted. He shook hands all around, kissed Daisy and told her he had a job for her any time we didn't treat her right. She laughed and said she'd remember that.

I saddled Ginger and rode a mile or so with him. When I reined up to go back, he said, "Lane, it's a funny thing how it worked out with us. I liked the cut of your jib when you first turned up in Miles City, but I never figured it'd be like it is."

His eyes were suddenly filled with tears. I was surprised, seeing this in a tough old bird like Tuck Loman. Then, just as suddenly and surprisingly, I felt a lump in my throat. Impulsively, I reached out again to shake hands with him as I said, "You come back and see us, Tuck. You hear?"

He nodded, gripped my hand, and started north again, then reined up. He said, "Lane, I don't know when it'll happen, but I know damned well with the kind of law we've got around here, that sooner or later we're gonna have to run some outlaws down or we're all finished. I'd like to know I could count on you when the time comes. Can I?"

I was too shocked to make a sensible answer. I said, "We'll see, Tuck."

I didn't really expect to have to make that decision for another year or more. I hadn't heard about any outlaws in the Yellowstone country since we'd come. It wasn't like the Black Hills, where the gold was a constant temptation to any man who didn't care about his morals. There were plenty of men like that on the frontier, but around here there just wasn't anything to tempt them, or so I thought.

192

By the end of October we saw we could let up. Morg had his horses broke and he rode into Miles City to see if he could sell them. Charley Higgins promised to buy them if they were as good as Morg claimed, but he didn't want them for another week or so. A rancher from the Little Missouri had just bought some of Higgins' stock, but he hadn't taken them yet and there wasn't room in the livery stable for more horses until they were gone.

I had been planning to help Morg drive his horses into town, but I'd also planned to move into town because the work had slacked up enough so I wasn't really needed on the Big D. At least I told myself that. The truth was the cold weather was at hand. We'd had a couple of light snows and I figured the transients would be moving into Miles City for the winter. I wanted to be on the scene when that happened.

I had a hunch Jake Rawlins would show up any time. Of course I'd had these hunches before and they had seldom turned out right, but I couldn't quit hoping. There just wasn't any other place in this corner of Montana for Rawlins to go for the winter.

After supper while Daisy was doing the dishes, I said as casually as I could, "I guess I haven't told you, but now that the work's pretty well caught up, I'm going to winter in Miles City. I'll ride back out here every month or so."

"Lane!"

She'd been standing at the stove with her back to me. Now she spun around, the single word jolted out of her. The light from the bracket lamp on the wall fell on her face. It was white, but now, as she stared at me, her face turned red. She moistened her lips and tried to say something, and couldn't. She started to cry.

"Hold on," I said. "There's nothing to cry about. I just told you I'd come . . ."

"Nothing to cry about?" she demanded, her voice so choked I could hardly understand her. "Don't lie to me, Lane Garth."

That shocked and angered me. I said, "I haven't lied."

"You're lying when you say there's nothing to cry about." She had full control of her voice then and the words rushed out of her in what was close to a scream. "You know damned well there's something for me to cry about. Why don't you come right out and say you're going to spend the winter looking for Jake Rawlins? You fool! You're possessed by him."

She threw her dishrag into the dishpan as hard as she could, some of the water splashing out and sizzling on the top of the stove. Whirling, she ran toward her bedroom door. She grabbed the knob, then stopped and looked back at me. "You can come here as often as you please, but don't expect me to sit here twiddling my thumbs waiting for you."

She ran into her bedroom and slammed the door behind her. I knew she'd be sore, but I hadn't expected this kind of outburst. She'd be here when I got back, I told myself. She'd put all of her money into the Big D. She had no other place to go. There wouldn't be any

194

work for her in Miles City. Then I remembered what Tuck Loman had told her. She must have figured on that when she said she wouldn't be here.

I went to bed, but I didn't sleep much that night. In the morning when I told Morg what I was going to do, he quit talking to me. Daisy cooked breakfast for us, but it was a sorry meal. She looked as if she had been crying all night. Leeper and Kelsey must have wondered what had happened, but neither asked.

There wasn't any use trying to make peace. We had simply reached the breaking point. I had known it would come sooner or later, but I hadn't foreseen it being as bad as it was. I put together a few things that I'd need, saddled Ginger, and tied the sack behind the saddle. I mounted, looking around for Morg, but I didn't see him. I looked for Daisy, too, but I hadn't expected her to be where I could see her.

I rode north, then glanced back, still hoping to see one of them, but I didn't. Then I got mad, as mad as I had ever been in my life. I should have knocked some sense into Morg and paddled Daisy, but that had never been my way. I'd let them alone, not really believing that Daisy would leave.

They weren't being fair to me. I told myself, as I had many times, that I'd been on Jake Rawlins's trail long before I had taken Morg in and even longer than the time when I'd first seen Daisy come out of the brush along the North Platte, her family lying on the ground in front of her, all dead.

I don't know what happened to me, or inside me, but

before I reached Miles City I was crying. I couldn't stop it. I had no reason to cry, or so I told myself. But I knew I did. For the first time I realized I couldn't lose Daisy. I had been telling myself all the time I wasn't in love with her, not the way I knew she was in love with me. But maybe I was. All I knew was that I simply couldn't bear the thought of not seeing her any more.

But I couldn't back away from Jake Rawlins and forget all about him, either. I was fully aware of this when I put my horse away in a livery stable and took a room over the Long Horn saloon. I'd go back to the Big D tomorrow. Maybe I could say something . . . do something . . . to make peace with Daisy and Morg. I don't think I really thought I could; they had been angry about this too long. But I had to try.

I ordered supper, but the food wouldn't go down and I finally pushed my plate back. I went into the Cottage saloon and had three quick drinks, something I seldom did. I didn't feel a thing from them. For all I knew, I might never get back to a decent relationship with Morg.

Maybe Daisy really would walk out. The hell of it was that I had known all the time it might work out this way. I had been too stubborn to think how I'd feel when it finally happened. Now I had a very strong hunch it was too late.

I went to bed and lay there, staring into the blackness and hearing the sounds that were normal in a saloon. I don't think I slept much until long after those sounds died down. I saw the first faint dawn light appear at the window, then I must have dropped off. It seemed only a few seconds before a fist pounded on my door, and Tuck Loman yelled, "Open up, Lane. I've got to see you."

I staggered across the room, rubbing my eyes and not even knowing where I was for a few seconds. I opened the door and saw Tuck standing in the hall. I said, "What the hell, Tuck, waking me up when I just got to sleep."

Tuck didn't apologize or ask to come in. He just said, "Get your pants on, Lane. A gang of horse thieves hit my ranch yesterday and stole twenty head."

"You can go after them without me," I said. "I aim to sleep a little more and then I'm riding back to the Big D."

"I think you'll ride with us," Tuck said. "Al."

Al Leeper had been standing in the hall. Now he stepped into view. "I came in for the doc, boss. He's on his way to the Big D now. I'm riding with Tuck and his men. That same gang of horse thieves hit us yesterday evening and stole the horses Morg finished breaking. They shot him up pretty bad."

"How bad?" I demanded, fully awake then. "Is he going to make it?"

"I ain't no doctor," Leeper said. "He lost some blood. Miss Daisy, she's taking care of him. Looked to me like if he stays flat on his back so he don't start bleeding again, he'll make it."

"Wait till I pull my pants on," I told Tuck.

"They're cooking breakfast for us in the Top Notch Cafe," Tuck said. "I'm having your horse brought over there."

He turned and walked toward the head of the stairs, Leeper following, their boot heels cracking sharply on the floor.

CHAPTER XX

By the time it was full daylight we were riding southeast: Tuck, Al Leeper, Charley Higgins, Tuck's foreman Les Johnson, and me. Tuck didn't know how many horse thieves were in the party. Neither did Al Leeper, but both said they thought there were at least three, maybe four. Even if there were more, Tuck figured we could handle them. Five good men were more effective than a big posse of men who were not dependable, he said.

The argument was an old one I'd heard before, but I knew that in general it was true. I had some reservations, though. Tuck said that if we were lucky, we'd catch up with the thieves this side of Powder River. If not, we'd probably have to go on to the Little Missouri where there were a number of outlaw hideouts and in that case we might run into a big gang of them.

By this time I knew Tuck pretty well. The way I judged him, he would not turn back until he'd finished the job. That was fine except that I couldn't see much sense in the five of us, good men that we were, taking on a gang of maybe twenty outlaws. I didn't argue, though. There would be plenty of time later on to argue if it came to that.

The day was a cold one. The sky was overcast and a strong wind was blowing down from the Rockies, bringing a few flakes of snow with it. We might be in a blizzard before we got back, a prospect that added to my concern. I took a good look at myself then, wondering why these fears were nagging me. It didn't take long to find the answer. I wanted to get back to the Big D before Daisy left.

I didn't know what I would say to her or how far I would go in making up with her, but I just couldn't get one thought out of my mind. I had to keep her on the Big D, for Morg's sake as well as my own. Suddenly I realized she wouldn't leave as long as Morg needed her, and then my fear evaporated and I stopped worrying about the size of the outlaw gang we'd tangle with or the blizzard we might be heading into.

We rode fast, taking only a few minutes out to eat the lunch we'd brought from the Top Notch Cafe. We reined up in a coulee where we were partly out of the wind, ate our sandwiches, took a drink from our canteens, and in fifteen minutes were on our way again.

Apparently Tuck hoped to catch the horse thieves sometime before dark because he would have brought a pack animal with supplies if he had expected to be gone several days. The lunch and filled canteens were all we'd brought. Tuck was running the show and we didn't ask any questions while we ate. We couldn't talk much as we rode. The wind sucked the words right out of our mouths and we had to yell to be heard.

About the middle of the afternoon we found snow covering the ground, just about an inch, but it was enough to hold tracks. I figured we ought to be cutting sign before long unless the outlaws had angled southeast as much as we had and were paralleling our route. I didn't think that was likely because the horse thieves would take the most direct route to the Little Missouri. They'd probably keep the stolen horses there and rebrand them, and maybe not try to trade them off until spring.

Of course I was doing some wishful thinking because there was a hole a yard wide in my thinking. The Little Missouri headed a long ways south of where we would hit it if we held to the direction we were taking. The hideout they were aiming for might be closer to the headwaters of the Little Missouri than where we'd hit it. If that was the case, we'd never cross their tracks until we reached the Little Missouri and rode upstream along its west bank.

About an hour later Tuck spotted tracks in the snow and signaled for us to rein up. He stepped down and studied them, then called to Al Leeper who dismounted and squatted beside him. They talked for a while, then rose and walked to where the rest of us sat in our saddles.

"If our men made those tracks," Tuck said, "and we think they did, we're mighty close to 'em. Ed and me both think they went through here about an hour ago. We can't tell how many riders are in the outfit.

They're moving fast, though. Chances are with the weather like it is they'll hole up on the Powder River. It's just yonder over them hills."

Tuck motioned with his right hand, his gaze moving from Higgins to Johnson to me and rested there a moment as if trying to figure out how I felt. He cleared his throat, then said, "If I've got my landmarks right, there's a deserted ranch on the Powder directly east of us. I ain't been there for more'n a year, but the last I seen it, the corral and stable and cabin were all in purty good shape. I'm guessing they'll spend the night there. What'll we do?"

Suddenly I felt their eyes on me as if waiting for me to decide. As far as I was concerned, I didn't have the least bit of doubt. I said, "Hell, Tuck, we don't have any choice. We'll go get them."

Tuck nodded and chewed on his lower lip a moment. He glanced up at the overcast sky and the tiny snowflakes that were being driven against us. He said, "I reckon so, Lane. We don't want to be caught out here in no blizzard any more'n they do. It'll be dark in another hour or two. Just one thing. That cabin is pretty solid. If they fort up inside, we'll never root 'em out of it."

"We'll get them," I said. "Let's ride."

Tuck nodded as if relieved, turned to his horse, and mounted. Leeper stepped up, too, and Tuck signaled for us to move on. He still led, but I began thinking about the way he'd looked at me, acting as if it was up to me to decide what to do. Suddenly it occurred to me that I'd had more experience manhunting than Tuck or the others, so I was going to be the leader whether I wanted to or not.

It bothered me. I just hadn't expected Tuck to perform this way. It had been his party back in Miles City. He had led all the way here, but now that we'd got to the place where the final decision had to be made, he was handing the reins over to me. If we caught the outlaws, we'd hang them. Not that I wanted to, and not that I believe in lynch law. We had no choice; it was simply the thing to do.

Half an hour later we were on top of the hill looking down on the Powder River. The light was fading some, but we could see the stable and the corral with the horses in it, and the cabin on beyond near the river. A sizable grove of cottonwoods stood a short distance upstream from the buildings.

"There they are, just like we figured," Tuck said. "What do you think, Lane?"

So it was my play just as I had expected. I said, "With the light this thin, I don't think they'll see us till we're there or nearly there. They'll probably have a guard out, probably in the stable or somewhere around the corral, but as cold as it is, he may not be very alert."

Tuck nodded. "That's what I was thinking."

"I'll take care of the guard," I said. "There's this ravine that leads right down to the corral. There's enough brush in the bottom of it that I can use for cover, so I think I can get to the corral without being seen. You take the others, Tuck, and circle till you get between the river and the front door of the cabin. I'll wait about ten minutes, then I'll tackle the guard if I can find him. If you're close to the cabin and can pull them outside, you can take them easy enough. They may come out if they hear any commotion at the corral."

"All right," Tuck said. "Charley," he motioned to Higgins, "you stay with the horses. Les, you and Al come with me." He hesitated, studying me for a few seconds, then said, "Lane, ain't you afraid you'll run into the whole pack of 'em?"

"I'm gambling on one thing," I said. "I don't think they'll expect anyone to be on their tail in this kind of weather. We've been moving pretty fast and we got a good start, so I'd say we're way ahead of where they'll expect us to be. Chances are they figure to move out early in the morning, thinking that if anybody is on their tail, they'll show up sometime tomorrow."

I had been thinking out loud as much as talking to Tuck, but now that I'd heard my own words, it seemed to me it stacked up pretty logical. Then I added, "It may make them look a little stupid, but it's my guess that most outlaws are stupid or they wouldn't be outlaws."

Tuck grunted something in agreement, then said, "It's your game. We'll play it your way."

I decided to wait the ten minutes here. I watched the three men angle north until they struck another ravine and turned down toward the river. We had to get the horse thieves, I told myself, before it was full dark. At least we wouldn't do any good shooting after it was dark. We could, of course, burn the cabin and force them out, but I thought that if we were lucky, we had enough time to wind this up before darkness blotted everything out.

Time is always hard to figure in a situation like this one, and I may have reached the corral sooner than I expected. Anyhow, I left the ravine and ran to the back side of the corral when I came down to it. I crouched there, listening.

I smelled cigarette smoke. A moment later I saw a man move out of the stable and stop at the corner of the building. "By God, Smokey," he said, "it's cold enough to freeze the balls off a brass monkey. The wind is worse'n it was when we rode in. Nobody's gonna be fool enough to chase us in weather like this. I don't see no sense in me getting myself froze . . ."

"Go on, damn it," a man inside the stable said angrily. "You don't know Tuck Loman. I do. He's only half man. The rest of him is bulldog. He'll ride in weather like this, all right. Now go on and look around. I'm going in and eat supper. I'll be out and relieve you in about half an hour."

The man who had stepped outside the stable started around the corral toward me, grumbling something about how even a bulldog wouldn't travel in this weather. I pressed back against the log wall of the corral and drew my gun. A few seconds later he came around the corral and saw me. At that moment he wasn't more than ten feet from me.

The man let out a high, hysterical squall and went for his gun. I was on him before he could swing his Colt up to cover me. I brought my gun barrel down squarely on top of his head in a brutal, down-striking blow that would have cracked his skull if he hadn't been wearing a hat. As it was he gave at hip and knee and went down, out cold.

I grabbed the gun which he had dropped and tossed it far out into the sagebrush. The man inside the stable apparently heard the squall. He may have started toward the cabin. I was too busy with the man I'd just slugged to be watching the other one. Anyhow, he didn't catch the tone of panic that was in the guard's squall, probably because of the wind and the racket the horses were making inside the corral.

Anyhow, this second man started toward me, saw me, and pulled his gun. I shot twice before he squeezed the trigger. My first bullet caught him in the right shoulder and turned him partly around, the second one drilled him through the head. I guess he was dead by the time he sprawled on the ground. At least he wasn't moving.

The cabin door was flung open and a man stepped outside, bawling, "What's going on out there?"

Tuck and the other two men had just rounded the corner of the cabin. Tuck didn't hesitate or order the outlaw to surrender. He simply shot him down, the man reeling away from the cabin doorway to fall face down into the snow. I started running toward the cabin as Leeper and Johnson plunged inside.

By the time I reached the door of the cabin, Tuck was inside, too. I heard a man shout, "Don't shoot. Don't shoot. I surrender. Don't shoot."

I was through the doorway in another ten seconds. A lamp was burning on the table. I saw a large man leaning against the far wall, his hands in the air. His face was covered by a thick growth of whiskers, but they didn't hide the long scar that twisted one side of his face. The second thing I saw was his peculiar build, his inordinately long arms and heavy shoulders that slumped forward. Instantly I was reminded of a great ape. In that second I knew I had at last caught up with Jake Rawlins.

Tuck still held his gun, the hammer back. He said, "Why shouldn't I shoot you, you horse-stealing bastard?"

"I ain't a horse thief," the man shouted. "They left me here with their extra horses in case a posse was crowding 'em. I was to have some grub ready and they were gonna eat quick and change horses and put their stolen herd across the river."

"How come we caught up with 'em?" Tuck demanded. "Or almost did? They ain't been here long."

"Not more'n an hour," Rawlins said. "They ran into a band of Cheyennes who thought they'd stole the horses from them. They had a set-to and lost one man before the Injuns had enough. That's what held 'em up."

Tuck started to raise his gun. I grabbed his right wrist and said, "No. Les, go fetch Higgins and the horses. Al, come with me. We'll find their horses and saddle two of them. Tuck, stay here and guard this son-of-a-bitch."

"Shootin' him would save us a lot of trouble."

"You don't shoot horse thieves unless you have to in a fight," I said. "You hang them, and you leave them for other horse thieves to see. You leave them hanging till their clothes rot off them and their meat drops off their bones."

"You can't hang me," Rawlins whispered. The strength to shout wasn't in him any more. "I was just waiting here for them men who had hired me to watch their horses. You don't have any reason to hang me."

"I've got another man beside the corral that I knocked out," I said. "We'll hang both of them."

Les Johnson and Al Leeper had already left the cabin. I turned to the door as Rawlins begged, "Don't hang me. My God, that's the worst death you can give a man. Go ahead. Shoot me, but don't hang me."

I looked at him, seeing my father lying there in the dust of our yard and my mother in bed, dead by her own hand because of what Rawlins and his men had done to her and to my father. I thought it was strange that this Jake Rawlins, who had left a trail of bodies behind him all over the Southwest and who had been a leader of outlaw gangs for years, had dropped so low that he had been left behind by a gang of horse thieves to cook them a meal and guard their extra mounts. Now he was begging us not to hang him.

"Don't shoot him, Tuck," I said. "He's killed men and women for years. You execute a murderer by hanging him, not by shooting him."

"Who is he?" Tuck asked.

"Jake Rawlins," I said. "He's not known up here, but to the south in Colorado and New Mexico and Arizona he's known very well."

Rawlins had stopped his babbling and was staring at me, his twisted mouth parted. "How'd you know who I am?"

I didn't take time to answer. I left the cabin, thinking he probably wouldn't even remember what he had done to my father and mother.

CHAPTER XXI

I lay on my bunk in the cabin most of the night staring into the darkness and listening to the snoring of the other men. It seemed to me that I'd been lying in bed and staring into the darkness quite a bit lately.

It wasn't the hanging of Jake Rawlins and the other horse thief that kept me awake. It wasn't the howl of the wind around the eaves of the cabin, either. Or the snoring. Tonight was different from the other nights. The thought that kept nagging at me was a good one. Maybe Morg was better. But the thought that followed wasn't good. Daisy might have decided that he didn't need her, and left the Big D.

We had finished the hanging before it was full dark.

We had taken care of our horses afterward by lantern light, and Tuck had finished cooking the supper Rawlins had started. We ate later, thinking it was a crazy kind of justice that gave us the horse thieves' food and bunks.

I had never had a part in a hanging before. I had always supposed it would make me sick and I'd throw up everything I had eaten for the last three days. It didn't hit me that way. On the other hand, it didn't give me any feeling of triumph or elation that I had finally reached the end of my long chase, that my father and mother were avenged. I was numb, I guess, because I didn't have any strong feelings at all beyond relief and the knowledge that now I could get on with living, real living with a purpose.

So I lay there, spent and tired, and understanding at last how Morg and Daisy had felt about my long chase. But there was something else, something I found hard to come to grips with, and that was my feeling for Daisy.

I'd had no time to think of love, no time to plan a future with a family. That had been the real waste and probably was the reason I had always thought of Daisy as a sister. I realized now as I never had before how much Jake Rawlins had been in my thoughts and my plans, so much that I had shut everything else out. Daisy and Morg had seen me do this. I had been possessed by Rawlins just as Daisy had told me.

How and what did I think about Daisy? She was eighteen, she was a mature woman because of the way she had been raised, because she had been left without any close relatives, because fate had thrown her in with me and Morg and she had become the woman in our family.

Did I love her? Did I want to marry her? How could I know so soon after I had dropped the noose on Jake Rawlins's neck and had given his horse a clout with my hat and he had been jerked out of his saddle to fall and pull the rope tight and snap his neck until he was dead?

I didn't know. I needed time. The problem was to keep Daisy from leaving the Big D so I could have the time I needed. I shut my eyes and tried to picture Daisy, tried to discover if I loved her as a man must love his wife. I couldn't. All I knew was that I had to get to her, to look at her, to hold her in my arms. Then I would know. I was sure of it.

One thing was certain. I could not stay here until daylight and spend the next day driving the horses back to the Big D. I got out of bed and pulled on my pants and boots and buckled my gun belt around me. As I lit the lantern, Tuck stirred and sat up in his bunk and stared at me.

"What are you doing?" he demanded.

"I'm going home," I said. "Al can help you with the horses. Figure on staying the night with us. We can cut your horses out the next day."

"Did you find some loco weed to eat?" Tuck demanded. "My God, man, you'll never make it in the night this way. You'll freeze to death. Wait . . ."

"All I know is I've got to go," I said. "I can't stay here. I'll make it."

I put on my hat and slipped into my sheepskin, then picked up the lantern and went outside, shutting the door behind me. The wind had died down. I saw there was about an inch of new, feathery snow on the ground, but it had stopped falling and the sky was clearing.

I strode to the stable, saddled Ginger, and blew out the lantern. Mounting, I rode up the hill to the west. By the time I reached the top, the stars were out. It was bitter cold, but the wind did not come up again, so the temperature was not hard to bear.

In about an hour the sky behind me began to turn pink and I knew I was still going the right way. I continued in the same direction, moving in as straight a line as I could toward the west, knowing I would hit the Tongue somewhere and hoping I would know which way to turn once I reached the river.

I found the Tongue when the sun was square over my head. The country was new to me, so I had hit the river south of the Big D. I turned north and within an hour rode into our valley. I saw smoke coming from the chimney, and a few minutes later I watched Daisy and Ed Kelsey cross the yard and go into the stable.

I was following the creek upstream toward our buildings when Daisy and Kelsey left the house. I didn't try to figure it out, but reined up in front of the house and ran in, wanting first to find out how Morg was.

Maybe, too, I wanted to put off seeing Daisy as long as I could. It would not be easy, it might not be pleasant, and I still did not know exactly how I felt about her or what I would say when I faced her.

Morg was lying on his back in bed, his face paler than I had ever seen it. He seemed surprised to see me. I asked, "How do you feel, Morg?"

"Weak as a day-old calf," he answered, "but I'll be all right. Lost some blood. That's all."

"We caught up with them on Powder River," I told him. "We got the horses back. The thieves are all dead."

He didn't seem much interested. He kept his eyes on me, boring into me as if trying to strip off my hide and see inside me, to discover how I felt and what I thought.

Finally he said, "I'm a man and Daisy's a woman, and we've grown up from being a boy and girl in the time since we first met you, but by God, Lane, I don't think either one of us know you. The trouble is you're two men. One of them is a crazy idiot who insists on wasting his life chasing a man he thinks he wants to kill. The other one is a hell of a good man and a hard worker who loves Daisy, but he's so stupid he doesn't know it. Now which one is the real Lane Garth, if you know, which I ain't sure you do?"

"I know, all right," I said. "I'm the stupid one who doesn't know he loves Daisy." It was an instinctive reaction to his question, but it told me something I had not been able to figure out myself, so, having said that much, I had to add, "I guess I'd better tell her."

"Then get a move on," Morg said. "She saw you coming and said she never wanted to set eyes on you again, so she asked Ed to take her into Miles City."

I went out of the house on the run. When I reached the stable, Kelsey had hooked up the team and Daisy was sitting in the wagon seat. She saw me, but she looked the other way. I reached up and grabbed her by the nearest shoulder and tumbled her out of the seat into my arms.

"You let me alone," she cried. "I'm leaving the Big D. I told Morg to tell you I never wanted to lay eyes on you again, so you just let me . . ."

There was one way to stop her angry flow of words and I used it effectively. I kissed her. I kissed her so hard and so long that when I finally released her, she stood looking at me, breathless and blinking her eyes, her lips trembling.

"Why, I didn't think . . ." she began, and stopped. "What did that mean? If it meant what I think it did . . ."

"It did," I said. "You are leaving the Big D, all right, long enough to go to Miles City and marry me. The hotel isn't much, but it'll have to do for a night or two."

She blinked some more, then she said, "I thought you didn't . . . I mean, you never . . ."

"Morg wanted to know if I was the stupid idiot who didn't know he was in love with you," I said. "I told him I was."

"I'll have to get my suitcase," she said. "I'll only be a minute."

"I thought you were all ready to . . ." I wheeled and looked into the wagon bed, but there was no suitcase or trunk. I yelled at her back, "You mean to tell me you were leaving the Big D without taking any of your things?"

She kept running toward the house, not saying a word or turning to look at me. I heard Ed Kelsey snicker and I started for him, then I stopped. No sense in bouncing him around. Daisy was the one, but that would have to wait.

I'd heard how deceitful women were. Now I knew it was true, but I decided to wait until the knot was tied good and tight before I told Daisy I was on to her.

Center Point Publishing
600 Brooks Road ● PO Box 1
Thorndike ME 04986-0001 USA

(207) 568-3717

US & Canada:
1 800 929-9108
www.centerpointlargeprint.com